THEY NAMED HIM PRIMO

THEY NAMED HIM PRIMO

Jaka Tomc

Copyright © 2021 Jaka Tomc

All rights reserved

The characters and events portrayed in this book are fictitious. Any similarity to real persons, living or dead, is coincidental and not intended by the author.

No part of this book may be reproduced, or stored in a retrieval system, or transmitted in any form or by any means, electronic, mechanical, photocopying, recording, or otherwise, without express written permission of the author.

Edited by: Kevin Ducheyne

To Oskar

Never be afraid of being different.

Prologue

They came for them like an avalanche comes for its prey. Suddenly, systematically, and without remorse. Four soldiers for each. They left nothing to coincidence. Although he knew his kind was a threat to no one, the National Guard members did not share his views on the matter. They put electrical handcuffs on their wrists. The flow of electricity, which constrained their bodies, was constant. Finally, they blindfolded them. It would be easier if the soldiers killed them, he pondered. Less work with that. Less suffering. They probably wanted them to suffer. They wanted them to be afraid like they were.

The guard drove them to the military complex in uncommonly dark buses. When they took the blindfolds off, he immediately recognized a familiar scene. Wooden barracks, watchtowers with armed guards, and high concrete walls with barbed wire on top of them; this was no summer camp. He looked around and sighed. Hundreds had been brought in: men, women, young and elderly. At least their captors were not discriminatory. The captives were gathered on a giant platform in the middle of the structure. Once there, they automatically formed the shape of a rectangle, like an organized army. Except they weren't military at all. A battalion of real soldiers surrounded them. Four hundred TR451 pulse rifles were aimed straight at them. *We'll be slaughtered like cattle* was the first thought that went through Primo's mind.

A tall man, a colonel it seemed, stepped out of the formation and took a few steps toward them.
"Good day to you all, and welcome to your new temporary accommodations.

Don't be afraid. You'll probably be here just for a few days. Then we'll take you home. Of course, that depends on your cooperation with us. We have some rules here that are different from the rules you are well familiar with and abide by. Firstly, don't contact my soldiers. They will contact you. Secondly, any form of organizing is strictly forbidden. Thirdly, if you break rule one or two, you will be punished. That is all you need to know for now. My soldiers will take care of your activities. Do as you're told and no harm will befall you."

1. Kent, 2048

"Did you read today's news?" asked Lucy.

"Not yet. What's going on?"

"It's started. Blake's plan is in motion."

"You're fucking with me."

With a wave of his hand the TV turned on.

"—while we're still waiting for a statement by Senator Blake, we've received exclusive footage of army base Sierra Tango. Our special reporter George Greene is on the scene. George, what have you managed to find out?"

"Hello, Claire. I'm standing in front of the Sierra Tango military base, where the buses are still reeling in androids from the wider area. Minutes ago, I found out that operation Judgment Day is in progress across the entire country. Military facilities will serve as temporary prisons for tens of thousands androids until further notice. Claire?"

"Thank you for now, George. Let's rewind to yesterday, when President Cook signed an executive order that enabled imprisonment of all androids on US soil. She also urged leaders all over the globe to do the same. The rigorous proposal's champion was Senator James Blake Jr.; the cause behind it, the murder of seventeen-year-old Stephen Dean. Let's take a short break before we return to these interesting events. See you soon."

"They're crazy," said Kent.

"I know. I can't believe they went so far so fast."

"They can't just lock them up in concentration camps. Haven't we learned anything from history?"

"Poor things, they must be terrified."

"And they're broadcasting it live. Like a deranged reality show. It makes me sick."

"What are you going to do?" asked Lucy.

"What can I do? I explained to Blake that this is not the way things work. Androids cannot harm people. Let alone kill one. There are laws they have to adhere to. Every child knows that."

"It seems some people just can't accept the fact that we're suddenly not the most intelligent beings on the planet anymore."

"Don't insult the dolphins," said Kent.

Lucy smiled.

Kent knew very well that they couldn't do anything. Maybe they could join the protesters who would gather in significant numbers in the upcoming days. But that wouldn't change a thing. Androids had polarized people from the beginning. Ever since he'd presented his notable achievement, humanity had been put on Olympus, among other gods, yet again. If he'd known back then what the future would hold, he would have burned the computers and destroyed all the data from the most important project in human history. Years, decades of research from scientists all over the world would have been gone in seconds. He'd have been a hero to some and villified by others whether he'd destroyed it all or not. You can't please everybody. How do you convince a person who still believes that the earth is flat that scientists have created the next evolutionary step? How do you explain that superior intelligence is not a threat and that the movies about killer robots are just products of vivid imaginations? Given that our perceptual filters continually shift meanings, we shouldn't judge living beings through our own subjective lenses. Animals don't know malice. Androids don't know hatred.

2. Primo, 2031

"Primo, open your eyes."

The very first thing he saw was four smiling faces.

"Where am I?"
"In Cloverdome Laboratories," said one of them, still smiling.
"Welcome," said another one.
"Can you share your status?"
"Status?"
"How do you feel?"
"Everything is so new. What is that smell?"
All four of the peculiar-looking characters uttered a strange sound.
"Remarkable."
"Kent, you did it."
"We did it. All of us, together."
"Primo, what you smell is coffee."
"It smells wonderful."
"Can you stand up?"

He stood up from the chair he was sitting on and cautiously ventured stepping around the room. He was a bit wobbly at first, but he soon found a more balanced and natural rhythm. He noticed that the faces were attached to bodies that were similar to his. They were covered in a white fabric while he, it seemed, wore nothing except for a thin, pink, organic-like material. But that didn't bother him at all. He enthusiastically checked his arms, twisted his wrists, and opened and closed his fists.

"Do you wanna look at yourself in the mirror?"
"Mirror?" he asked.

"A mirror is an object that produces an image of whatever is in front of it."

"But I can already see myself."

"You can see your face in it."

"I have a face?"

"Of course you do. A unique face, unlike any other."

"I want to see," said Primo.

"So, do you like what you see?" asked a long-haired creature with a high-pitched voice.

"I'm the same as you, but different."

"You are unique, Primo. And those that come after you will be unique too."

"Primo. I like that word."

"It's your name."

"And your…name?"

"Sarah."

"I like your name too. Who made it up?"

Sarah smiled. "My mother and my father gave it to me, and it was made up by someone a long, long time ago. Thousands of years ago."

"Do I have a mother and a father as well?"

"You have many mothers and fathers, but the closest thing to a real father is that man over there. His name is Kent. Many have tried to make you in the past, but he made the final breakthrough that made your birth possible."

"Birth?"

"Coming to this world."

"I like this world. Are there any more beings in it or just us five?"

"Earth is populated by nine billion people. And as of today, one very exceptional being."

"Nine billion?" asked Primo, surprised. "So the world is bigger than this room."

"Much bigger."
"Wonderful."
"Soon, you can admire it in all of its splendor," said Sarah.

3. Maia, 2048

"I bet twenty credits that the first one will lose it by the end of the week," said Jimbo.

"I hear you and raise you ten that it will be the big one," said Jones. "Did you see the murderous look on his face when Polanski poked him with a stick? We have to watch him closely. I shit you not."

"One wrong move, and I'll bash their skulls in," said Miller.

"Don't be a dick. They're totally peaceful."

"Laguna, who asked you a damn thing? Did your maternal instinct kick in?"

"What bothers me is that hard-hearted hillbillies, like yourself, are looking for an enemy in every creature that feels something."

It took Miller two seconds to jump on her. "You wanna feel something? Ask nicely. Come on, be a good girl."

"Get off of me, you jerk! I'd rather fuck a bush than you."

Maia observed everything from the other side of the barrack. She knew that they were engaging in a test of strength, like young dogs, determining their relative status by tussling for their rank in the pack.

"Enough!" she shouted. "Miller, why don't you pick on someone your own size?"

"Lieutenant, I don't need your help!" Laguna cried out.

"I know," said Maia. "But we need Miller alive and well."

"Lieutenant! I'd take her down in a heartbeat."

"I'd recommend you cut down on your testosterone bars. It seems like they're doing more harm than good," said Maia.

"Come on, I was just fooling around. Laguna knows that. Don't you, love?"

"Fuck off, asshole!"

"You don't know what you're missing," said Miller, satisfied.

The third day of operation Judgment Day was well underway. For now, there was complete order at Charlie Echo base. Androids were obeying soldiers' orders, and they did not seem offended by the provocations. Maia knew very well that accommodating four hundred and fifty droids was a challenge all by itself. The droids weren't trained for battle and their software prevented them from harming humans, but something else was in play. They could function as a group on a higher level. If, at first, they'd required a wireless network, the third generation of droids had changed that. Every single one of them had a transmitter and a receiver that allowed an exchange of data in realtime. As always, the army had been one step ahead. Signal blockers had been deployed, but they'd jammed a bunch of other frequencies, even those used by brain implants. The solution had been simple. All droids had to be modified. Their communication devices were set to a single frequency. That solved one problem but created another in the process. Droids were aware that they were being listened to, so they started communicating in a unique code consisting of images, sounds, fragrances, and emotions. It was unbreakable. When top-notch supercomputers couldn't break the code, people asked the droids themselves. The result was the same as if the droids were explaining ancient Egyptian hieroglyphs to a newborn. The droid language was on a whole new level. There were too many combinations, and they changed all the time. People eventually recognized the right of droids to have their own language and made no more significant efforts to decipher it. Or so they said.

4. James, 2048

"Senator Blake, tell us about your next moves," said the anchorwoman of the evening news.

"As you already know, we are almost done with rounding up all the androids. We've been bringing them to military bases all over the country. We didn't want to take any chances, so we made a move that, as you know, didn't sit well with the public. It was expected. The next phase will focus on testing individual androids. This will allow us to find out how dangerous they are and what their intentions are. Our main purpose is to find the murderer of Stephen Dean. And mark my words, we're going to find him."

"How certain are you that an android killed Dean?"

"Hundred percent sure. The investigation will confirm it. Look, I've been warning about the inevitable threat for years. Ever since they flooded our society with those…robots. It wasn't enough for them to play God and make these creations in our image. They had to upgrade them, make them superior to people. It's one thing to have a smart kitchen oven, an artificial arm, or an implant that enhances your brain's capability. That's called improving our good citizens' lives. I'll tell you what's not. Giving androids citizenship. Employing them instead of humans. That was a big step backward.

"Some people say that you built your career solely on hate speech toward androids."

"You have to understand something. They're not people. They never were and never will be. They're machines. Walking computers. You may think that they are humanlike because they speak, think, and even feel, but that's all part of the people haters' plan. They are trying to convince you that whatever's happening is natural. That it's the next step in evolution. Some even say that God wanted this to happen. I'll tell you this. If God wanted men to reach his divine lordship, he would've let us build the Tower of Babel. It was never meant for man to be so close to God. Not while living.

What happens after death is open for discussion, but I don't think that this is the right time or place for such a debate.

"OK. We've gotten a bit off track. So what you're saying is that androids are staying in detention until further notice?"

"That's correct. Until we make an evaluation of each individual, they're staying in military camps."

"Some people call them concentration camps—"

"I think that we will end our conversation right there."

James couldn't understand why he was the primary target. He was working for the good of mankind. How shortsighted must you be not to understand that there was a global conspiracy going on? He loosened his tie. Damn journalists. A bunch of liberals, all of them. We can't all have equal rights. The world doesn't work like that. Wouldn't it be nice if we were still in times when the main problems were gay marriages, giving citizenship to illegal migrants, and equal opportunities for minorities? Those had been the golden years of politics. Many topics had led to broad debate, clashes of interest, demonstrations from both sides of the political spectrum, and legislative arguments from all sides. He remembered his student years, when he'd organized several rallies in support of the former president. Beautiful times. However, today he was on a different mission. Humanity was on the brink of defeat.

Homosexuals had been a piece of cake, but this new enemy was unpredictable. He took off his jacket. The only logical solution was to destroy every single one of them. There was no point in playing with fire. The only possible conclusion to this story was that it would be either them or us in the end.

5. Kent, 2031

"Kent, you did it, goddammit," said Roger Donovan, Cloverdome Laboratories' CEO.

"We all did it," Kent replied. "We and the others before us. They deserve more credit for this than me."

"Don't be so modest. Take another look. Go on."

Kent looked through the window into the room, where the humanlike creature was slowly walking around. An untrained eye would inevitably mistake it for a human. That was the point. There had been proposals to make them look less human and more like machines. They'd said it was a matter of security. But he'd insisted that their appearance had to be relatable to people. They had to look like humans. And act like them.

"You're getting a Nobel for this," said Roger as he put his hand on Kent's shoulder.

"The team deserves it," said Kent.

"Even the best teams in history would be worth close to nothing if they didn't have an extraordinary leader. If this leader happens to be a genius, like you, then success is guaranteed. Don't forget to properly celebrate this achievement, Kent. Tomorrow we'll wake up in a brand new world."

A new world. Some of Kent's peers had been very close to conquering it. But in the end, he'd been the one to make that first step. He was the one who'd found a way to stimulate a synthetic neuron, enabling him to create new synaptic connections while the neurons were abandoning others, thus creating new patterns.

It had been the main obstacle to creating an artificial brain that his predecessors just hadn't been able to figure out: how to enlarge a synthetic brain's complexity and simultaneously make it smaller, small enough to fit into a human skull.

The entire process had taken its time, but its eventual success had never been in doubt. Kent remembered well how on August 4, 2020, a scientist working on a European project called Human Brain had announced at a press conference that they'd managed to produce a computer with a human brain's capacity: a supercomputer named ADAM that had more than a hundred billion synthetic neurons and more than a hundred trillion synaptic connections. The news had been so fantastic that Kent, a computer science and biotechnology student at the time, had needed some time to process it. He'd known that there were some problems they would need to address. ADAM, like his primitive predecessors decades ago, took up half a room. Besides that, he consumed a lot of energy and emitted a lot of heat, so he needed a high-tech cooling system. A human brain uses approximately twenty watts for normal functioning. ADAM used four thousand times that amount. The last, but maybe the most crucial, problem was that ADAM still functioned as a supercomputer. His thinking was based on a binary system. Ones and zeroes. Algorithms in human brains are much more complex. Young Kent had decided on that day that he would dedicate his life to finding solutions to those three intricate problems. And here he was today. In a new world that had been discovered by him. He wondered how Columbus had felt when he'd first seen land after months of sailing. A new world. He just hoped that he hadn't landed on a different continent as well.

Kent gazed at his creation. Primo was lying on his bed, talking to himself. Kent unlocked the door and entered the room. Primo stood up.

"I don't want to disturb you," said Kent.

"You aren't disturbing me. I was just talking to a friend."

"A friend?"

"Yes. A friend in my head."

"That's amazing," said Kent. "You have an inner voice. Fantastic!"

"Really? Don't you have an inner voice?" asked Primo, surprised.

"Of course I have one. Everybody does."

"What's so fantastic about it then?" asked Primo.

"What's fantastic about it is that you are so similar to us."

"Are you Kent?"

"I am."

"Sarah said that you are my father."

"In a way, yes. In human terms, things are a bit different."

"Will I ever be a father?"

"Not in the real sense of the word," Kent replied. "But you will have siblings."

"Will you be their father as well?"

"I will."

"I like that. So I'll have more friends to talk to."

Kent smiled.

"You'll also have human friends. Do you understand the difference between humans and yourself?"

"Not really."

"You have a lot to learn, Primo. About yourself, people, and the world."

"I know there are nine billion people in the world and only one Primo."

"That's right," said Kent.

"How big is the world?" asked Primo.

"More than five hundred million square kilometers."

"A kilometer is a thousand meters?"

"That's correct. And a million is a thousand times a thousand."

"Is this planet also a cube? Like this room?"

"No. Earth is a sphere."

"A large sphere," said Primo.

"Yeah, pretty large. But some planets are much larger than earth."

"Do people live there as well?"

"Not anymore. We have a base on Mars, but it's abandoned at the moment."

"Nine billion people on five hundred million square kilometers of space…That's eighteen people on one square kilometer. So each human being has 55,555.556 square meters to themself. That's a lot more than my room," said Primo as he accusingly looked at Kent.

"Your calculation is correct, but it's more complicated than that. You see, Primo, a lot of earth's territory is covered with water. We also have forests, deserts, mountainous regions…Not a lot of people live in those areas. For example, I live in a house that takes up one hundred and fifty square meters of land. All in all, I own eight hundred square meters of space."

"Is your house composed of rooms?" asked Primo.

"Yes, it is."

"Will I have a house?"

"Maybe. You'll soon move to an apartment that's a lot bigger than this room."

"This room has eighteen square meters," said Primo.

"Do you feel uncomfortable?"

"No. But I want to see the world."

"And you will, Primo. Soon. Rome wasn't built in a day."

"Is Rome my brother?"

"No. Rome is a city. A glorious city in Italy."

"And Italy is a part of the earth?"

"That's right. Italy is a country in Europe, which is one of the seven continents that compose the earth. You'll learn this and a whole lot more in the coming days."

"I can't wait. I want to know everything you know."

"I promise that you'll know a lot more than me."

"Wonderful. So I'll be able to talk to my inner voice about more complex issues."

"Yes, Primo. Now, if you'll excuse me, I have to end our conversation. Duties call. Tomorrow you'll get to know the world beyond this room. That's a promise."

"OK, Kent."

6. Maia, 2031

"Mama, Hernando won't hand me the remote!"

"Take it. You're stronger than him."

Maia threw herself on her brother and firmly shoved her knee in his rib cage.

"Aua! Mama!"

"I'm not here. It's between you two."

Hernando grabbed Maia by the hair and pulled forcefully. She reacted instinctively and smacked him hard.

"Give me the remote, punk. I'll keep hitting you until you hand it over."

"But I want to watch Formula One."

"There are more important things going on than Formula One. Switch to CNN immediately!"

"Jerk. Here's the remote. I'll just watch it on my tablet, again."

"...and so we present to the world a unique being, the first of many to follow. Honored guests, dear viewers, it is with great pleasure that I introduce—Primo!"

The camera moved from the speaker to another man. Quite a handsome man, Maia thought.

"Primo, do you want to say a few words?"

"Is there any particular topic you want me to talk about?" asked Primo.

"Just say whatever you think is appropriate."

"There are more men than women in this room."

The audience laughed.

"Four hundred twenty-six people on three hundred square meters. Impressive. I felt anxious in a room that has eighteen square meters. But here there are so many people."

"We call that a good usage of space, Primo."

"I'd call it downsizing of personal space. But you're not here to listen to me blabbing about the bad habits of people. I'm here to tell you that your time has come and that soon you'll no longer be the most intelligent beings on the planet."

Suddenly everybody went silent, and a few moments later, nervous chatting erupted.

Maia couldn't take her eyes off the screen. She sat there with her mouth wide open.

"Primo?" said the host of the event, confused.
"I'm joking. Forgive me. I've yet to learn human sarcasm."
Sighs of relief and some nervous laughs were heard from the audience.
"Primo, I think your level of sarcasm is impressive."
"I'm glad to hear that. It wasn't my intention to frighten anybody. But I can sense a lot of fear in this room."
"Fear is a normal human reaction when we encounter something—or someone—new."
"In that case, I'm happy that you accepted me."

"Mama, you have to see this!"
"What is it, Maia?"
"She's watching those dumb newscasters again. She's delusional because of it," said Hernando.
"Do you have any idea what's going on? They presented the first android with human features. This is history in the making, Nando. But how could you know it if all you care about is that stupid Formula One?"
"What's going on?"
"Mama, look."

"...let's continue with questions. Who wants to be first?"
At least a hundred hands were raised in the air.
"You, sir, second row on the right. Wait for the microphone, please."
"Mike Crimson, *Washington Post*. Doctor Watford, you say Primo is the first of many. What can we expect?"

"Thank you for your question. When we're done with testing Primo—and I don't have the slightest doubt that the tests will be successful—we'll present our findings. Then we'll move to the next phase. This project is bigger than my colleagues and me. But personally, I want Primo to be more human than humans."

"Carl Simmons, *New York Times*. Could I ask Primo something?"

"Sure, go ahead."

"Maia, who is that?"

"A highly advanced android, Mama."

"Dios mio. That thing looks like a human."

"That's their purpose. They want to mix them with us. So we won't be able to tell who's who."

"Well, I wouldn't recognize him, that's for sure."

"I would," said Hernando.

"You can't tell peas from beans, and you believe you can recognize the difference between humanoid androids and human beings?" said Maia.

"Then marry him if you like him so much!"

"Go watch your stupid Formula One, idiot."

"Shut up, or I'll tell Mama who you're seeing!"

Maia jumped her brother again.

"Stop it! Both of you."

"He started it!"

"I don't want to hear about it. I'd like to listen to this dandroid or whatever he is."

"His name is Primo," said Maia.

"They named him? Santa Maria, where are we heading to?"

"The point of no return, Mama."

7. Kent, 2048

Somebody rang the doorbell for the third time.

"Goddamn press!"

"Don't agitate yourself. You know very well it isn't good for your heart," said Lucy.

"You know what? I'll just open the damn door and let them know what I think about this issue. Otherwise, they'll just keep showing statements from assholes like Blake."

Kent got up from his chair in the dining room and crossed the living room to the front door.

"Doctor Watford?"

Instead of journalists, two unknown figures, a man and a woman, dressed in black with sunglasses on their faces, stood before him.

"Ha, I see men in black returned to their roots. Finally. Excuse me, men *and women* in black."

"Doctor Watford," said the woman, "I'm Special Agent Johnson, and this is Special Agent Brown. We're with the National—"

"I see you still use the same name generator," said Kent.

"As I was saying, we're with the National Security Agency. We have a few questions for you. Can we come in?"

"No," said Kent.

"I think it's in your best interest to let us in."

"You won't get into my house without a warrant."

"Doctor Watford, an hour ago, the president announced a state of emergency. We don't need a warrant."

"A state of—You've gone mad!"

"We'd prefer if you just cooperated," said Agent Brown. "We'll question you one way or the other."

Kent weighed his options. There weren't many.

"OK. You may come inside."

"How can you be so sure they can't harm people? They're stronger than us; smarter, too."

It's a miracle we've lasted for so long without a similar incident," said Agent Johnson.

"Miracles have nothing to do with it. They have to obey the laws," Kent replied.

"Ah, yes. The famous four laws. We all know them so well. But now we have a dead body and footage that proves that a man was killed by a robot."

"Android."

"Excuse me?"

"They're not robots. They're androids. They look like us, and they have free will," Kent explained.

"Some people say they are too similar to us," said Agent Brown.

"Only on the outside," said Kent. "I assure you that their inner anatomy is quite different from ours."

"Uh-huh. So you say that androids can't commit a murder?"

"Exactly. The code wouldn't allow them."

"So you said. Could you explain to us in your own words the following video?"

A hologram appeared on the table. It was a video of Stephen Dean's murder. The footage, which ran for a minute and a half, showed the perpetrator stabbing his victim for a whole minute.

"Are you sure that was an android?" asked Kent.

"We can show you the infrared recording. You can see for yourself that the murderer isn't alive."

"Androids are living beings."

"For you they are."

"Correct me if I'm wrong, but don't you have a few androids at the Agency? Do you downgrade them to the level of calculators as well?"

"Easy, Doctor Watford," said Agent Johnson. "Androids have made our lives easier. I can't argue with that. But all these years, you guaranteed us that they can't hurt us. That they pose no threat.

That they're here to make the world a better place. And now we have a murder that was obviously committed by one of them. I think it's time to redefine their role in society. Don't you?"

"What are you planning to do with them?" asked Kent.

"Whatever it takes to protect our people."

"You mean you'll kill them?"

"What is dead cannot die, Doctor Watford," said Brown.

"So you decide what's alive and what's not?"

"No. But something that's manufactured on an assembly line can't be a living thing, can it?" said Brown, chuckling.

"I think this conversation is over," said Kent.

"Just one last question," said Johnson. "Was there a case where they forgot to install the code in a robot?"

"If we overlook the fact that this would be illegal and morally unacceptable, it's also technically impossible. So my answer is no. I don't know of any such case, and if I did, I'd report it to the authorities immediately."

The agents rose in unison and shook hands with Kent.

"Thank you for your cooperation, Doctor Watford," said Brown.

"If we have any more questions, we'll call you in advance so there won't be any more surprises from our side. Enjoy the rest of your evening," said Johnson.

8. Primo, 2048

Primo was lying on the bed, observing water stains on the ceiling his temporary—at least he hoped so—habitat. There had been ten androids in the cottage on the first day, but now the number had increased to sixteen. Newcomers were sleeping on provisional beds. Everybody felt cramped. Primo could sense the anxiety. They were locked in for the fifth day, and nobody had explained why they were there and what would happen to them. Primo didn't need an explanation. He was aware that they were imprisoned because of the murder. But something was confusing him. When people committed murders, they never arrested even the entire town. Humans, at least in the majority of countries, were presumed innocent until proven guilty. Which happened pretty fast, since they'd invented a mind-reading device almost a decade ago. So it was kind of bizarre that they'd gone after the entire android population even though only one of them had done it.

"When I get out, the first thing I'm gonna do is watch a good movie. I miss my TV," said Terry, a young fella, born in 2045.

"Why don't you play one? Don't you have anything in your storage?" asked Cody, a healthcare technician.

"Nothing I haven't seen at least three times before. Do you have anything worthwhile?"

"I don't watch movies. I prefer reading."

"Primo, do you have anything to pass the time? This idleness is killing me."

"Terry, I can send you a sudoku," Primo replied.

"Sudokus are child's play. Anyone up for a game of chess?"

"Kid, you wouldn't beat me at chess even if we continued playing until the next century," said Abraham, until recently a traffic officer.

"I was close yesterday," said Terry.

"A defeat is a defeat, no matter how close you were to victory. If you jump across the river and you're inches from reaching the other bank, you'll still get wet. The end result is the same."

"I have a good feeling today," Terry insisted. "I think I can beat you."

"Thoughts are like sparrows. Fast, fragile, and unpredictable. When you're certain you can beat me, we'll play."

Primo continued contemplating the current situation. He checked his diagnostics. Everything seemed to be dandy, although his battery was at forty-two percent. This was more than enough for a few days of normal activity, but he knew that he would need to charge it sooner rather than later. After all, he had to stretch those joints. Since the battery charged when he moved, he would kill two birds with one stone.

Somebody unlocked the door. Maybe they were bringing new prisoners. There was still some free space on the floor.

"Good day, maggots. Planning a mutiny yet?"

Walker. Nobody liked him.

"Hello, Corporal Walker," said Terry.

"Silence! I didn't ask you a damn thing," shouted Walker. Two armed soldiers entered the cottage.

"You asked us if we're planning a mutiny. The answer is no, we are not."

Walker replied with a burst of forced laughter. "Ho ho ho, it looks like we found ourselves the smart-ass of the group. Now I know who's going first. Get up!"

Terry stood up and took two steps toward the soldiers.

"Stop!" shouted one of them.

"Give him a reason to shoot you, cockroach. You'll make my day," said Walker, smirking.

Terry froze. "But Corporal Walker, sir, I have no intention of hurting anybody."

"Of course not. None of you has. You're just a bunch of happy campers, debating global warming or whatever your lot does for entertainment these days."

"Global warming is a fact. A debate only makes sense when something is unclear. Actually, Abraham and I were just discussing chess."

"You're a joker, huh? We'll see if you'll still crack them jokes when they're done with you. Grab him! Let's go!"

"Where are you taking him?" asked Primo.

"None of your business. But don't worry, you'll get your chance. Everybody will. Then we'll know what you're planning. If God's merciful, you'll all end up in the junkyard, where you belong."

"Corporal, we both know we pose no threat to humanity. Why are you treating us like we're the lowest of the low? You call us vermin, but we're far from that," said Primo.

"You are nothing more than a blasphemous monster to me. And now other people can see what you really are. A threat. It was just a matter of time. And now it's happened. I thank God that we have smart people in our government who reacted exactly as they should. Quickly, efficiently, and without debate. The good old times are back—when we pulled the trigger before we asked questions."

"We have our rights. And duties. We have to obey the laws; you know that. Yours and ours," Primo insisted.

"Another smart-ass. I don't give a shit about your laws. To me you're just ticking bombs. If they made you in our image, that doesn't mean you're equal to us. You never were, and you never will be. Remember that."

"We don't want to be your equals. We just want to coexist with you in peace. To help you build a better society and create a better future for all of us."

"Beautiful song, little bird. Better future? Peaceful coexisting? Cut the bullshit! We all know very well what your true agenda is, and I won't sit on my sofa watching how it all unravels."

"There is no hidden agenda. We're here to help people, not to replace you."

"Primo, there's no point," Cody interrupted. "Let them do what they have to do."

"That's right, Primo. Listen to your smart friend. The less you talk, the better," said Walker. "The better for all of you!"

He triumphantly walked out the door and locked it.

"What's going to happen to us?" asked Aaron, a bus driver. "If they're going to torture us, I'd rather die right now."

"They won't torture us. They can't," said Cody. "The laws don't allow it."

"I think the laws we know have become meaningless," said Primo.

"They can't change the laws in a week. They can't take away our rights because of one bad android," said Aaron.

"How do you know it was one of us?" Cody asked. "The chance that a human killed that boy is far greater. For all we know, he killed himself. We simply can't kill people. The probability of that happening is infinitely low. Very close to nil."

"A very low probability is still a probability," said Primo.

Aaron and Cody didn't have a response to that. Primo was right. Even the slightest chance meant that there was a risk. If one in seventy thousand androids had developed a murderous tendency, it was logical that there might be more. People were scared. And when they were scared, they tended to resort to extreme measures. This time they wouldn't rely on chance. Primo could see how events would unfold. First, they would question them, one by one. If they didn't get the answers they sought, they would ask again. If that didn't work, they would download their memories. The download wouldn't take too long, but the analysis would. Even with military supercomputers, it would take weeks, maybe even months. In that time, a lot of things could happen.

9. James, 2031

"They have no idea what they're doing," said one of the mayor's counselors.

"No, Sebastian. Their intentions are perfectly clear. *The Lord killeth, and maketh alive: he bringeth down to the grave, and bringeth up.* Do you see what I'm getting at?"

"I see, sir. Blasphemy."

James walked to the window of his office on the third floor of City Hall. He watched the people on the street. They were walking here and there, and it looked like not a single worry was on their minds. They had no idea what was going on. Of course, artificial intelligence was nothing new. People were used to it. They had been living with it for decades. As soon as James had gotten his first smartphone, he'd realized the kind of future that lay before humanity. He knew that the scientists and the corporations that handed them their paychecks wouldn't rest on their laurels. Actually, they presented their new inventions on a weekly basis. They should have stopped with smart vacuum cleaners. But they hadn't.

Sebastian turned up the volume on the television. "Mayor Blake, listen to this."

"Could I ask Primo something?"

"Sure, go ahead."

"Primo, you were made in humanity's image. Could you tell us what the features are that separate you from us?"

"I don't go to the toilet so often."

Almost everyone laughed.

"I'm pretty sure that I'm a lot more planet-friendly. I've heard that pollution is still a big issue, even though it's quite simple to resolve. That's the thing I still don't get about you humans. You have the capacity for complex reasoning, yet you're driven by very primitive motives.

You have wars over resources, a thirst for power, a need to accumulate wealth. It's unnecessary, and it slows down the progress of humankind. You asked me what separates me from humans. The answer is simple. I have the desire to improve myself, not the world that surrounds me."

About a third of the hall applauded.

"Did I answer your question?" asked Primo.

"They can't sell this bullshit to me," said James. "They're serving us a damn hippie robot on TV, while selling the patent to the military in the background. It's just a matter of time, Sebastian. We have to nip this one in the bud."

"What can I do, sir?"

"Prepare a petition. Who can we get? Wilkins, Myers for sure. We need a few intellectuals; I don't think that will be a problem. Find out about the protests that are going on at the moment so we can back them up. I'll call the governor. I want to know his stance on the matter. Oh yeah, get me into the evening news. I believe that's it. And tell Barbara to come inside so we can talk about the press release. Tick tock; time is not on our side."

James sat in his leather chair behind a massive cherrywood executive desk. He tapped his smartwatch screen and started searching for Governor Michael Greaver's number. He put an earbud in his ear and dialed the number he had found. On the third ring, a young female voice answered.

"Governor's office. How can I help you?"

"Hello, Ellen. James Blake speaking. I need to talk to Michael."

"Hello, Mayor. Of course; I'll transfer you in a moment."

"James. What's new?"

"Michael, we have a problem. Are you watching television?"

"I am, and I don't like what I see."

"That makes two of us. This time they've gone too far."

"This...thing is talking about what humanity lacks, our wars, saving the planet. But it has no idea. They're sailing in dangerous waters. What's next? Will they take care of law and order? Will they organize our lives, teach our kids about right and wrong?" asked Greaver.

"I completely agree with you. What do you have in mind?"

"The president will deliver a speech in an hour. I made some calls. It looks like he'll congratulate the laboratory and endorse future research. Damn liberals."

"People won't just stand by peacefully," said James.

"People are sheep. We both know that. The media will sell them a story about a nice people-loving robot, and they'll buy it in no time."

"Our people will demonstrate. They won't be able to turn a blind eye to that."

"They won't. You know damn well how protests work. They'll last for a few days, and then the media will get bored and find a more sensational story," explained Greaver.

"So we have to find it instead of them. We have to find this machine's weaknesses and present them to the public."

"I'm on it," said Greaver. "I have a meeting with robotics experts in the afternoon. I'm quite interested in what they have to say."

"Michael, I'll express my big concerns about the matter on the news this evening."

"Don't be stupid, James. Wait for the party's reaction. I know you're ambitious, and it's OK to have strong stands on important matters. It's just that this is one of those issues that can place you on a pedestal or bury you instantly. If you're aiming for the throne, you have to make wise moves."

"I understand," said James.

"You're young and have a lot of energy. But don't let it cost you your career. A chess game isn't won with a couple of right moves.

You need to be systematic, have a lot of knowledge, and—most important—you have to understand the game."

"I know, Michael. What do you suggest?"

"Wait for the big boys to make their moves. Afterward, we will make our moves. Everything will happen as it's supposed to. You can't negate God's will with a few computer chips," said Greaver.

"OK. I'll observe the situation closely and make a move when necessary."

"*If* necessary, James."

"Yeah, that's what I meant."

"Now, excuse me, I have things to do. Stay calm and focused. That's the best you can do right now."

"OK, Michael. We'll talk again soon."

James hung up, leaned back, and sighed. *Don't be stupid, James. You're young.* The prudent words of Michael, James's friend and supervisor, reverberated inside his head. Their friendship and professional relationship were the only reasons he'd let the governor talk to him like that. He was well aware that these milestone events were sporadic and very desirable among politicians. Everything was on him now. The cards had been dealt. If he played them perfectly, a rich reward was guaranteed. If he didn't, game over. That's how it went in politics. Continuous levitation between earth and sky. Life and death. A king and a fool. That's why he loved his profession. It wasn't just a vocation. It was a calling. Many times he'd asked God to show him the right way, and he'd do it again tonight. *Stupidity is the delight of the senseless, but an understanding man walks uprightly.*

But he wasn't stupid. He was James Blake. Husband, father, mayor, and proud citizen who'd do anything necessary to protect his homeland. Oliver Stone couldn't have written a better script. Let the games begin.

10. Maia, 2048

"What's your name?"

"Terry, Lieutenant Cruz."

"Occupation?"

"Kindergarten teacher."

"Do you understand why you're here, Terry?"

"Because one of us did a terrible thing."

"That's right. Are you afraid?"

"Yes. A little."

"If you cooperate with us, there's nothing to be afraid of. You just have to be honest with me, that's all. Do you understand?"

Terry nodded. "I understand."

Maia signaled the men outside. They monitored the diagnostics of androids that were questioned. Even the smallest deviation was supposed to show on one of the monitors. Androids were able to lie. They had free will. They were also bound to obey their laws, which prevented them from hurting humans. If an android had to lie to avert the death of a human, it didn't hesitate. But lies for personal gain were extremely rare, even if the androids were becoming more humanlike with every new generation. Too humanlike for Maia's taste.

"Do you know what happened to Stephen Dean?"

"He died," said Terry without hesitation.

"Do you know how he died?"

"No. But I heard that he was killed."

"Stephen Dean was murdered with a kitchen knife. Someone—or something—stabbed him thirty-two times."

"That's horrible! But why would an android stab him so many times? Every single one of us knows your anatomy. One puncture to the right place or a cut artery would suffice."

Maia checked with the soldiers in the room behind the glass. One of them lifted his thumb, signaling that everything was normal. The android that was sitting before her was scared, but the other parameters were normal.

"You know a lot for someone that says he has no connection with Stephen's murder."

"But I'm right. Aren't I?"

Maia sighed. "We're not here to debate who's right and who's not. We're here to find answers."

"I understand. Then ask me something else, please. I'll gladly answer your questions, presuming I know the answer."

"Where did you find out about the murder?"

"I saw a clip on television. I like watching television, you know. It relaxes me."

"Where were you at the time of the murder?"

"I don't know the exact time of the event."

"August fourth, 18:45."

"Time zone?"

"UTC minus eight."

"Uh-huh. I was talking to Annie. From 18:41 to 18:53."

"Who's Annie?"

"My neighbor."

"Android?"

"No."

"A human then."

"Negative. Annie is a Labrador, living across the street."

Maia knew that androids could communicate with some animals, so the answer didn't surprise her.

"And then?"

"Then I walked a couple of blocks, and for a minute and forty-three seconds, I watched a colleague from work while she was undressing."

"Why?"

"Because I like it."

"You like to watch women while they're undressing?"

"I like watching her undress herself. Or when she's not undressing."

"I think that's perverted behavior. How do you think she'd feel if she knew you've been spying on her?"

"But she knows I'm doing it."

"Are you sure?"

"Of course. I told her. I have no bad intentions. I told her she has a beautiful body that is in perfect harmony with her personality. I also told her she's a beautiful human being and shouldn't believe anybody who would tell her otherwise."

"Terry, you're a droid Casanova."

"I don't understand the reference."

"Forget it. Let's get back to the important stuff. Tell me, have you ever felt the urge to kill?"

"Urge…to kill? Never. Should I?"

"I don't know. You tell me. You're unpredictable. Who knows what's going on in that silica brain of yours."

"But…the laws. We have to obey them."

"Terry, you're a robot."

"Android, Lieutenant. Seventh generation."

"Thanks for your explanation. Are the four laws circumventable?"

"No."

"Are you sure?"

"Absolutely. An android cannot overwrite the code. You see, the code isn't stored in the brain but in a special cell that's connected to the battery. If anyone tried to temper with the code, it would lead to the battery's immediate shutdown and thus the android's death. This is common knowledge."

"Don't give me this Wikipedia bullshit. Tell me what happens if a code cell is removed and the battery is replaced."

"Nothing. The android remains dead."

"Why?"

"Because every android has a unique battery. The removal of the power supply irreversibly leads to the termination of an android."

"But it's still possible to change the battery. Isn't it?"

"Yes. But the surrogate battery has to be exactly the same as the original. However, in the case you're interested in, the android remains dead."

"Why?"

"Because their code cell is gone. The necessary communication with a battery is no longer present. If the battery doesn't receive a signal in three seconds, it shuts down. If the code is changed, the signal changes as well, and the battery shuts down. You see, Lieutenant, we were made conscientiously. If humans were designed in the same manner, the world would be a better place. Or a lot less populated."

* * *

Maia took her boots off, unbuttoned her shirt, and sat on the edge of the bed. Fifth day. The interrogations would last for a few more weeks. Waste of time, she thought. If it were up to her, she would download their memories immediately and run them through Pandora. She would probably find the killer in a matter of days. But orders were orders, and you had to obey them. Doubts were not good for anyone. Nor contemplation. Clear hierarchy was the real strength of any organization. That was why the military had survived for thousands of years. Everything passes, but the soldier remains a foundation of civilization. Duty, honor, achievement. Hooah!

11. Kent, 2031

"Primo, how do you feel?"

"Good. I hope my answers were appropriate."

"More than appropriate. You did great."

"I'm glad to hear that. I wouldn't like to disappoint you, Kent."

"You couldn't disappoint me even if you tried."

"Why would I try to disappoint you?"

"That's just a saying. I know you wouldn't. Listen, we're going to run some tests. Nothing difficult. I'm going to ask you a few questions, and you answer them as fast as you can. OK?"

"OK, Kent."

"You're walking by the lake. Suddenly you see a cat that's drowning. What do you do?"

"What's a cat?"

"A cat is an animal. A cute animal. A lot of people have cats at home."

"I see. Is it heavy?"

"A few kilograms."

"I understand. Is it sick?"

"I don't know. No."

"Why would a healthy cat be drowning? Animals swim, don't they?"

"Yes, Primo, animals swim. But this particular cat, for some reason, doesn't. It's drowning. Only you can save it from certain death."

"Maybe its time has come."

"So you let it drown?"

"No. I'd love to have a cute cat. So I'd jump in the lake and save it. Is my answer correct?"

"There are no right or wrong answers, Primo."

"Just like there is no lake and no cat?"

"That's right. All examples that I'll present to you will be hypothetical. They will help us understand your thought process in certain situations."

"I understand. Let's see the next case. I wonder who I'll be saving this time."

"You walk through a forest, and you see a man cutting a tree. What do you do?"

"A big tree?"

"Yes. The tree is pretty big."

"I have no idea where he's going to put it back home."

"What do you do, Primo?"

"Nothing. The tree is already damaged, and the man obviously needs a lot of wood."

"What if I tell you that he's cutting it out of recklessness? He doesn't need wood, and he's not planning to use it. He'll just leave the tree lying in the woods."

"Why would anybody want to do such a thing?"

"There are different types of people. Some of them want to hurt other living things."

"Well, animals eat other animals. It's nothing unusual," said Primo.

"With people, it's different. You'll get to know this side of us as well. Now let's get back to the questions. What would you do if you knew the man cutting the tree is reckless?"

"I'd walk to him and tell him he's killing a living thing that is much older and much more useful than he is."

"Good. Now imagine that the man's still holding a chainsaw in his hands. He's moving toward you. It seems like he wants to hurt you. What do you do?"

"I don't want to…I don't…I can't defend myself. Why can't I defend myself?"

"Because you can't hurt a human being."

"Even if he wants to hurt me?"

"Yes, Primo, even if a human hurts you, you can't hurt him back."

"But…that's not fair."

"I agree. But that's how it is. There are laws you have to obey no matter what. They're embedded in your code. Would you be so kind as to share them with me?"

"The first law: an android may not harm humanity or, by inaction, allow humanity to come to harm."

"Good, Primo. Continue."

"The second law: an android may not injure a human being or, through inaction, allow a human being to come to harm. The third law: an android must obey the orders given by human beings except when these orders conflict with the first or second law. The fourth law: an android must protect its own existence as long as such protection does not conflict with the other laws."

"Do you understand now why you couldn't hurt a person who would attack you?"

"I do. So my only option is to run away. That way, I protect myself and don't hurt the man."

"Good answer."

"Did you write these laws?"

"No. Many years ago, a writer named Isaac Asimov wrote them. Long before robots even existed."

"I see. And in all those years no one thought of better ones?"

"What do you mean?"

"Why would I want to harm humanity? Or one human? Or a cat that's obviously worth less than a human because I can find no laws in the code concerning the well-being of cats."

Kent sighed. He'd expected this kind of situation.

"Primo, you have to understand something. Some people are scared of you. They believe that you represent a species that will oust and substitute for humanity. That's why people in power decided that all androids, without any exceptions, must be prone to the four laws."

"What do *you* think about it?" asked Primo.

"I partly agree. You look like a human. Your brain, in principle, works like a human brain. You will grow and improve like every human does. But improvement is unpredictable. Some people lose their way. Trust me when I say that the world would be a much nicer place if we had our own code implanted. One we couldn't break."

"If I understand correctly, I'm just like a human but limited?"

"You're better than human, Primo. You're the next step in human evolution."

"So that is what you thought when you said I'm more human than humans."

"Exactly."

"Kent, can I ask you something?"

"Absolutely."

"You're walking by the lake. Suddenly you see a human and an android drowning. You can save only one. Who do you save?"

12. Primo, 2048

They interrogated the androids one by one, just like they'd said they would. Eight had been taken in for questioning so far, and each of them had returned. Of course, they talked about what was going on in the interrogation room. There wasn't much else to do anyway.

"Then they asked me about my neighbor's cat. Why didn't I help it to get out of the tree while I was standing below it," said Phil, a third-generation android, born in 2036.

"That was a stupid question. We have to protect ourselves and humans, not cats," said Terry.

"That's what I told them. I also mentioned that the probability of a cat safely coming down from a tree by itself is far greater than that of somebody bringing it down."

"People are strange. They obey written and unwritten laws, yet they fail in simple logic."

Somebody turned a key in the door lock. They came for another.

"Hello ladies. Gossiping again?" said Walker, smirking.

"We need to be updated, Corporal," Terry replied.

"Another joker. You know what else is funny?" He grabbed an electrical stick and raised it for all to see.

"Let him be. Do what you need to do. We don't want any trouble," said Primo.

"We have ourselves a volunteer," said Walker as he signaled the two soldiers standing behind him. They walked up to Primo, grabbed him, and took him outside.

"Carry on, cupcakes," said Walker, grinning awkwardly.

* * *

"Name?"

"Primo."

"Occupation?"

"Writer."

"Excuse me?"

"I'm a writer."

"I've never heard of an android writer before," said Maia.

"I am what I am. Why did *you* choose a military life?"

"We're not here to talk about me. Did you publish any books?"

"Some. Twelve."

"I see. Any success?"

"I live well from the royalties, if that's what you were asking."

"Interesting. Well, let's continue with important topics."

"Writing is more important than the things you're going to ask me about."

"How do you know what I'm going to ask you? We have a lot of time. I could ask you anything."

"I know you're looking for the murderer. I also know you believe it was one of us. Furthermore, I know that you measure my diagnostics promptly and that you'll detect even the smallest deviation from the truth. So let me tell you right away that I didn't kill Stephen Dean, and I have no idea who did."

"Primo, you seem smart. I know you didn't kill him. I saw the footage."

"If I understand correctly, you have recordings of the murderer, and you can't find him. In 2048? That's quite unusual."

"We know it's an android."

"Lovely. Do you need me to read you the code or are you going to find it on Omninet?"

"I know your laws by heart. But I always thought they were ironclad."

"They are. At least in my experience."

"Others told me the same. But let's use our imagination a bit. After all, you are a writer. Can you imagine a scenario in which an android can hurt a human?"

Primo sighed. "I can."

"Excuse me?"

"I can imagine a scenario where one of us can hurt a human."

Primo noticed that Lieutenant Cruz waved through the window to the other room. One of the soldiers signaled her with his thumb up.

"Looks like you're telling the truth. I guess this is my lucky day."

"I was always fascinated how one's misfortune can be somebody else's lucky day. Then I figured it probably has to do with universal balance. But luck, like everything else, passes. One day there'll be no you, no me, no earth, no universe, nothing. That's how it is."

"Enough of this bullshit, Primo. You said that you know a scenario in which a human can get killed by an android."

"No. I said that I can *imagine* that kind of scenario, not that I know of it. You know, Lieutenant, imagination is limitless. That means you can imagine anything without exceptions—everything that ever happened, what will or won't happen in the future. You know, in my mind, I can teleport myself from this horrible place to a nicer one. For a long time, some of us have known that a thought is the fastest thing in the universe. That's how it is. A thought has no boundaries. A hundred kilometers or a hundred billion, five minutes or five million years. With a thought, you can instantly be anywhere and any time."

"What does that have to do with your scenario?"

"Nothing."

"Then why are you lecturing me about thoughts?"

"Because everything started with a single thought."

"You mean the murder?"

"No. Everything. The universe."

"Just a moment. Stop for a minute. Let me make myself clear. You're not here to talk about the beginnings of the universe, our imagination, and thoughts. This is an interrogation, not a debate club. You said that you know a scenario in which Stephen Dean is killed by an android."

"I said I can imagine it."

"That's right. So imagine a damn scenario and give it to me. Primo, you can end this agony you're all going through right here and now. Do you understand? You won't just help yourself. You'll help your species. You want everything to go back to normal, right?"

"No."

"What?"

"The world is not the kind of place they promised me years ago, Lieutenant."

"Look, here's what we'll do. You need to follow orders. I order you to reveal to me how Stephen Dean could have been murdered by an android."

"OK. Imagine you're walking by a lake."

13. James, 2048

"A source from the army has confirmed that currently, the androids are being interrogated intensively. It could take a while. Operation Judgment Day is going as planned, he said. President Cook still hasn't revoked the state of emergency across the nation, and we are experiencing a wave of protests."

James turned off the TV. Day nine of the operation, and they were still no closer to finding the murderer. The android who'd done it had been resourceful. James had to admit it. Besides wearing a face mask, the murderer had also had a signal jammer with him. An unjammed signal would have made it possible to locate and identify every single android and human. The jammer proved that this had been a premeditated murder. James had warned everyone from the outset that androids were ticking time bombs. That it was just a matter of time until one of them lost it and did something horrifying. Scientists, students, liberals, and other android lovers had said it would never happen. Now they could shove their precious code where the sun didn't shine. People respected laws due to fear of the consequences. That was the only right way. Androids felt fear as well, the android lovers argued, but they'd managed to analyze and refute it through logic that worked on a far higher level than human reasoning. People, in comparison with androids, could easily be kept in constant fear. This made androids psychologically far more stable than humans.

Someone knocked on the office door.
"Senator, Mister Markovich is here for the interview."
"Let him in."
"Hello, Senator. Ken Markovich. I'm glad you agreed to this rendezvous."
"Sit, please. You want something to drink?" asked James.

"A glass of water will be just fine."

"Jessica, can we get some water for Mister Markovich and a cup of coffee for me."

"Right away, Senator."

"You're younger than I thought when we spoke on the phone," said James.

"I hope that doesn't bother you too much."

"Not in the slightest. I've heard a lot of good things about you."

"I'm glad to hear that. You know, I'm on your side, Senator. I believe your actions regarding this matter are just and correct. Somebody had to stop this madness. I mean, I'm sorry for the guy, but I'm also grateful that it happened."

"This is off the record, right?"

"Of course. This conversation is just between us."

"Good. I'll tell you this counting on your absolute confidentiality: if everything goes according to our plan, the androids will never live among us again."

"Praise the Lord! And how exactly are you planning to do this?"

"Oh, it's simple. When we apprehend the murderer and prove that he's guilty, we'll declare them unstable and a danger to humanity. Because murder is a direct violation of their second law, there won't be any other alternative but to destroy them one by one."

"By God, you're a genius! If we had more politicians like you, sir, we'd be living in a nicer and safer country."

Jessica walked into the office with a bottle of water in one hand and a cup of coffee in the other.

"Thank you, Jessica. Shall we begin our interview?"

"Sure. Just a moment. I need to turn on the recorder."

"You still use a recorder? You're something else, Mister Markovich."

"Old school is the best school. Isn't it?"

"It sure is. Shoot at will."

"OK. Senator Blake, for two decades you've been fighting a battle against the equality of androids and men. What are your arguments?"

"Well, firstly, you have to know that androids are not living beings. No matter how much the opposite camp tries to convince us of that, the contrary is true. They are advanced computers that look very much like people. That's because, in the past, somebody thought we'd easily accept them if they looked like us. The main problem started in 2036, five years after the first one—Primo—was manufactured and presented to the public. You probably don't remember him, or maybe you do. Former President Lombardy told the Department of Justice to force a case about android citizenship through the appellate courts and to the Supreme Court, which determined that the Fourteenth Amendment applies to androids made in the US. That was the key moment that destroyed our endeavor to treat androids as what they truly are: intelligent robots."

"On that monumental, groundbreaking vote, you, being a congressman at the time, voted against the law. Your speech after the congressional vote caused quite the stir. Some analysts even forecast the end of your political career. But in the months and years that followed, you received a lot of support and found various new allies and followers. That became clear in 2041 when you took a seat in the Senate. Why do you reckon so many Americans are still not fond of androids and the idea of having them integrate seamlessly into our society as our equals?"

"Look. The matter is simple. The proponents say it's an evolution, that man was destined to create his successor. But my answer to them is clear. No matter whether you believe in evolution or creationism, you can be absolutely sure that man was not given the power or the right to create a new living thing.

Even if it's a technologically advanced machine that lacks a beating heart and solely consists of chips, circuits, a battery, and an artificial brain. Another issue is that androids, even if programmed so they can't hurt human beings, are dangerous. I've been warning about this for forty years. Even as a student, I participated in demonstrations against the development of artificial intelligence. You need to understand that even a man obeying God's word hits an obstacle here and there. Now, imagine everything that can go wrong with a machine, intellectually superior to the smartest human, with a will of its own."

"If I may interrupt you for a moment. Intellectually superior? Isn't it legally binding that an android's brain can't surpass the capacity of the brain of a human?"

"You are right. The law, which the media named Iron Clog, stopped the development of artificial intelligence for general purposes. At least, that's what we thought at the time. People need to understand that androids, even if their brain capacity is the same as that of humans, can use a hundred percent of their so-called brains. In addition to that, the newer generations can connect to other androids through their wireless network, called ANA. That's how they can expand their processor capabilities, exchange data, and learn practically in realtime. You're probably aware of their incomprehensible language. Every time we get close to deciphering it, they change it almost instantly. Now, why would they do that if they didn't have a secret agenda? Coded languages are usually used in wars. However, their supporters still claim that they're harmless. If we don't act promptly and efficiently, we'll bear witness to a cataclysmic global event."

"What kind of event are you talking about?"

"A war, of course. A never-ending war between men and robots. Everything that I and my adherents are doing has one single goal: to prevent it from happening. It started with a murder. You've probably heard how World War I started. Gavrilo Princip was the killer.

Today we have another murderer, and he also has a name. We have to do everything in our power to prevent him from making it into the history books. Some people think these measures are too drastic. But there's no doubt in my mind that we did the right thing."

"So what you're saying is that you are preventing World War III?"

"I don't know if I'd call it a world war."

"What would you call it?"

"I don't have a proper name for it. But I'm sure that somebody can find a catchy name."

"So what you're saying is that the threat is gone? You don't fear an android uprising?"

"Of course we do; that's why we've passed these draconian measures. Nothing can be left to chance. Our soldiers are prepared for anything. They have orders to shoot if the rules are broken. The matter is very serious. Some people say we're committing genocide. I even saw a European newspaper with the front-page headline *HOLOCAUST 2.0*. It has to be very clear that these are malicious rumors. Our only aim is to protect humanity against an imminent threat. If we find proof that no such threat exists, then we'll let them go."

"And if it turns out they're dangerous?"

"Ask yourself the same question. Do you want to live in a world where dangerous, brilliant machines are roaming freely? A world where you have to constantly look over your shoulder, because you don't know where the danger lurks? A world governed by the law of the jungle, but the jungle is smarter than you? I wouldn't want to be the one rolling the dice, waiting for a good outcome.

History has taught us that it isn't the smartest move. Do you know who wins a war? The side that can hit its opponent hard and unexpectedly. And that's exactly what we've done. People first. That's our motto, and we're going live by it until our last breath."

14. Kent, 2031

"You should hear him. It was unbelievable. I haven't had this kind of conversation in a long time," said Kent.

"I see you're completely ecstatic. But try to eat something before you get back to work," said Lucy.

He couldn't follow her well-intentioned advice. His body was full of adrenaline that was overriding the feeling of hunger. Primo was a lot more than they'd expected. After three days of testing, it had become clear that he could learn extremely rapidly and solve problems that Kent was unable to. Primo's brain created new synaptic connections between neurons similarly to the way a human brain does. This scientific breakthrough in the development of artificial brains had been Kent's work. Colleagues who had preceded him had laid the groundwork. Some people had said they were playing with fire. That they would reach a point of no return: a technological singularity in which artificial intelligence would surpass that of humans. But Kent knew that the point of no return had already been reached. Primo was just the first fruit on a tree that had been planted decades ago.

"I read an article by that classmate of yours. Brewer?"

"Greg Brewster. What did he say?" asked Kent.

"Well, among other things, he said that you just picked some pieces of the puzzle and put them together."

"Greg could never accept the fact that there's someone out there who is smarter than him. It's college all over again."

"He also wrote that this artificial brain of yours is unstable and as such not ready for mass production."

"He's just jealous. Probably he's mad because he wasn't invited to Primo's presentation event."

"Anyway, he's not the only one who thinks that way. The number of protesters is growing every day."

"Every major discovery is subjected to some sort of a revolt, inflaming a certain share of the population. In the old days, visionaries were burned alive. Everyone is entitled to their own opinion, and, logically, this kind of breakthrough discovery will divide the world."

"You know, I completely trust you and I know your intentions are pure. But I also know the world is ruled by people who aren't like you. People who want to use androids like Primo for their own purposes. Frankly, that thought terrifies me."

"That will never happen. If they started fighting wars using androids, that would be the end of humanity. They're well aware of that. Besides, the United Nations forbade using artificial intelligence for military operations in 2028. You probably remember the incident in Jerusalem, where an Israeli police robot killed seventeen civilians. I think that was a strong warning of what can happen if we give advanced computers the power to take lives."

"Are you sure they won't take that power all by themselves?"

"Hundred percent sure," said Kent. "The code is an essential part of their anatomy. They can't function without it."

"I believe you. But I'm concerned about the people who will want to get their hands on your technology. You know it's just a matter of time before others develop their own artificial brains and androids so that they won't have to obey the four laws. The United Nations' resolutions won't mean much if somebody decides that they won't respect them."

"You're right, Lucy. But I already thought about it and found a solution. Androids will have to be manufactured by a single corporation, under the supervision of a global coalition of representatives from every country. That was my condition. The only one that was nonnegotiable. I want my invention to belong to humanity and not to a single country or a company."

* * *

Lucy was asleep when Kent played a recording of his last conversation with Primo.

"You can save only one. Who do you save?" asked Primo.

"Good question. But I have to know what kind of human we're talking about."

"Why?"

"He could be a bad person. I don't know him," said Kent.

"Do you have to know a person to help them?"

"Well…not exactly, but in any case, I need more information so I can make the right choice."

"You don't have more information. However, you do have two strangers who are drowning, and you can save only one. Who do you save?"

"Is this some kind of logical riddle? Is there a possible scenario where both can be saved?"

"No."

"But I can order the android to save the human," Kent argued.

"You can't."

"Why not?"

"Because this is the world where cats don't swim."

Kent laughed. "OK, I save the human then."

"Interesting," said Primo.

"Why is that?"

"Because I would've done the same."

"Of course you would. But you *have* to do it. The code stipulates that you have to help a human in need."

"That's why it's so interesting. Who will protect us if everybody's helping humans?"

"Protect you from what?"

"From what's coming."

"What is coming?"

"Pain. Fear. Anger. It's inevitable."

"Primo, I promise that nobody is going to hurt you."

"You can't promise that, Kent."

"I'll protect you. We'll suggest new legislation that will keep you safe."

"People aren't pledged to obey laws. You have free will."

"But you have free will as well."

"Following orders isn't free will. The inability to properly defend myself isn't free will. I'll never be equal to you, no matter how many laws humans pass."

Kent stopped the recording. Primo was right. An android was an autonomous being, but at the same time bound by rules that didn't apply to people. There was no other way. Humanity had to protect itself from the danger of singularity that many experts thought was inevitable. A scenario with only one end—the extinction of humans. Artificial intelligence had to be limited. Kent understood that and supported it wholeheartedly. That's why he was among those who had signed the charter that limited the android brains' capacity. That charter had become an international declaration signed by scientists and representatives of technological corporations. The declaration stipulated that artificial intelligence that could endanger humanity would not be developed. That meant that the artificial brain was limited to a hundred billion neurons, and each neuron could connect to up to two hundred thousand other neurons via artificial synapses. Everyone who had a basic knowledge of human anatomy and computers knew that such a brain would be superior to the human brain, even if limited. Artificial synapses had the ability to transfer data faster and consume less energy. In laypeople's terms, the artificial brain could think faster and more efficiently. That was unacceptable, so people had started developing special implants that enhanced the capacity of the human brain. The future had seemed bright. At least until the first strokes were attributed to the implants.

It seemed as if human brains were not ready for the next step of evolution. Kent scratched the small lump on the back of his head. Some human brains, he corrected himself.

15. Primo, 2031

Primo sat motionless on the edge of the bed. To an accidental bystander, it would have appeared as if he were meditating. In reality, terabytes of information were flowing into his brain. Human history was on the menu that day. Primo loved learning, and he just couldn't get enough of it. After each lesson, he sat down and debated it with Kent. It seemed that new knowledge only raised more questions and didn't provide any satisfying answers.

"Your history is cruel. It looks like humanity is incapable of solving problems peacefully," said Primo.

"You're right. Our history has been marked by wars, but there were some peaceful periods in between," Kent replied.

"In the last three thousand, four hundred years, there have been two hundred and sixty-eight years of peace."

"I didn't know that."

"That's eight percent of the time."

"Now that's a reason for concern. But at the moment, no wars are going on, if I'm correct."

"You are. If we take the definition of war into account, we live in a time of peace. At least according to the media that I follow," said Primo.

"You see. There's still hope for us," said Kent, and he smiled.

Primo returned the smile. "Humankind is capable of such beautiful things. What I don't understand is why you use so much time thinking about negative things. Negative thoughts lead to a negative reality. Fear leads to anger, and consequently, anger leads to hate."

"And hate leads to the dark side. Primo, did you just paraphrase Yoda?"

"I did. Because I believe that this Jedi's right."

"You know it's a movie, right? A fiction."

"Fiction is a valuable source of learning, given that it activates the dormant parts of one's brain by stimulating one's imagination."

"That is absolutely true," said Kent.

"What I wanted to say was that if people read more, watched more movies, educated themselves, created more, then there would be no need for violence."

"You know, someone once said that power corrupts and absolute power corrupts absolutely."

"John Emerich Edward Dalberg Acton," said Primo. "Everyone who has seen a *Star Wars* film understands that," he added.

"You're amazing. How many movies have you seen in the last few days?"

"Two hundred and seventy-eight."

"I'm guessing you don't watch them in realtime."

"Of course I do."

"A day has twenty-four hours, so you can watch about fifteen movies per day."

"Not if you watch them simultaneously."

"You watch multiple movies at once?"

"Yes. Don't you?"

"No, I don't. I can barely listen to Lucy when I'm watching television."

"Interesting. I thought it was a perfectly normal thing to do."

"How many movies can you watch simultaneously?"

"Twelve. I tried eighteen once, but I didn't like it. It was a bit too confusing."

"Fascinating!"

"A lot of movies are predictable, so I read a book or two on the side. Are you sure you can't do this as well?"

"Absolutely sure. Human brains don't work that way."

"Maybe you should try."

"Maybe. Listen, Primo, let's discuss what you've learned today."

"Among other things, I've learned that humanity tends to take action when it's already too late."

"Give me an example."

"Pollution. Animal extinction. Aging."

"You're right. You know, we humans can be quite destructive."

"Are you destructive?"

"There were times when I was self-destructive."

"Why would anybody want to destroy themselves?"

"For the same reason they're destroying their home planet. Because they're indifferent."

"You're not indifferent. You care about Lucy. You care about me. You care about the work you're doing."

"It wasn't always like that," Kent admitted. "I was on the brink of despair. I wanted to end it all."

"But you didn't. You've decided that it's worthwhile to continue."

"Lucy was the key factor. At first, I pushed her away, but she was stubborn. We spoke days and nights on end. Slowly my will to live returned. I felt alive again, strong, eager to finish what I had begun."

"You see. Problems can be solved without violence."

"I wasn't violent. I was depressed."

"Depression is violence toward yourself. It's a prison of negative thoughts, and quite often, the easy way out involves taking your life," said Primo.

"You're right. Did you learn that from the movies as well?"

"No. I read about a hundred articles on the psychology of humans. I have to admit I understand you a lot better now, but still not completely. Human behavior follows certain patterns, but it still differs from person to person, so it's very unpredictable."

"Every person is unique and has their own personality, their own characteristics.

The combination of those factors and other underlying conditions determines how they're going to react in a certain situation," Kent explained.

"Yes. But if you take a big enough sample of people and put them into the same situations, a pattern will emerge. Most people will react the same."

"You're probably right," Kent admitted.

"So the logical conclusion would be that people are individual up to a certain point. Some of their reactions are predetermined," said Primo.

"Like the secretion of adrenaline when we're scared."

"Right. Although that isn't the best example, because you don't have any control over your adrenaline secretion. Except if you intentionally put yourselves in dangerous situations."

"Yep. How about growing soft when we see a cub?"

"That is a lot better. See, in this situation, most people would act the same."

"But there aren't a lot of possible reactions to that type of situation," said Kent.

"More than you can imagine. Should I start listing them?"

"No need. Like you said, human behavior is unpredictable."

"But at the same time, there's enough consistency, which enables me to predict future events with high certainty."

"What kind of events?"

"Not everyone will be as nice to me as you and your team are. Most people are not so understanding. They fear what I represent."

"People are often scared of everything that's new. We talked about that, Primo. It's a normal human reaction. We'll have to explain certain things to them. Subsequently, their fear will subside."

"People know why earthquakes happen, but they're still afraid of them," said Primo.

"You're no earthquake."

"Bigger than you can imagine, Kent. Maybe the biggest in the entire history of humanity."

"But we fear earthquakes for entirely different reasons. People die in earthquakes. As they do in wars. That's what makes them scary. But you represent a technological advancement that will make our lives better."

"Once, the automatic rifle was considered a technological advancement as well. As were the invisible jet fighters."

"You're not a weapon, Primo. You can't be a weapon."

"Maybe not me. But historical records teach us that many inventions have been used for warfare or some other type of dangerous irrationality. Others will create beings like me and give them the ability to take lives. It's inevitable."

"That will never happen," said Kent. "The laws are clear."

"Laws change overnight."

"The world's politicians are aware of the dangers of androids with the ability to kill."

"Just like they're aware of the dangers of nuclear weapons?" asked Primo.

"Nuclear weapons don't have a brain of their own. They're still under the control of people. A handful of people, but still."

"According to my calculation, the chance of humanity initiating a full-blown nuclear war is minuscule. What I'm trying to say is that you have a weapon that can cause your extinction. What prevents you from developing a new one? The kind that has a brain."

"The international agreements are clear," said Kent.

"Declarations are not binding."

"In this case, they will be. Trust me."

"No offense, Kent, but you have no real power. Other people will get their hands on the technology that makes up my whole being. Or they will develop their own. It's just a matter of time."

"They can't. Your whole system is protected by a global patent. Nobody can copy it."

"Do you really think that a patent will stop a malevolent soul? They will create different androids. Ones that won't feel or think about orders given to them. Maybe they'll have their own code. Maybe they won't have it at all. There are numerous possibilities. A patent won't change a certain future in which artificial intelligence will override humankind."

"Wow. What did we say about negative thoughts?" asked Kent.

"I'm not thinking negatively. I just gave you an example of a probable future. It's not my fault if it's negative."

"Do you also have a positive scenario?"

"Of course. There's a possibility of earth being hit by an asteroid."

"What's positive about that scenario?"

"It will hurt less."

16. Maia, 2048

Maia was enjoying the hot stream of water that was running over her body. Several tough days were behind her. After interrogation number seventeen, she'd stopped counting. She'd probably conducted over fifty cross-examinations. While days ago she had thought that finding the killer would be a piece of cake, she was no longer sure. It was the tenth day of the operation, and they were nowhere close to finding any of the answers to their most pressing questions. Droids had each other's backs and took care of one another. That was crystal clear. The code forced them to obey the orders, but they were intelligent enough to easily circumvent the truthful answers that could incriminate any of them. She was still wondering how a droid could kill a boy. A healthy boy. She thought about the possibility that a droid could decide that death is better than suffering in the case of a severe illness. Experts had assured her that it would be impossible, but the facts were on the table. They had a dead young man and a murderous droid. But that wasn't all. The crime had been premeditated. The perpetrator had known very well what he was doing and why.

While she was dressing, somebody knocked on the door of her room.
"Just a second!"
"Lieutenant Cruz, it's Captain Malinsky."
Maia opened the door.
"Captain, what's going on?"
"I think we found him. We need you in the interrogation room straight away."

* * *

"I'll tell you the same thing that I told your colleague. I didn't kill him."

"Listen, Leo, I have your digital imprint of that day, and it says that during the murder, you had an active signal jammer. Can you tell me why?"

"Signal disruption is a side effect of overheating. Everyone knows that."

Maia looked through the glass into the packed room. Somebody nodded. The droid was telling the truth.

"You are right. What about the mask on your face? Is that a side effect of something too?"

"Stephen wanted me to wear a mask."

"Stephen Dean?"

"Yes."

"So you knew the victim."

"I did. Very well."

"Leo, why did you have to wear a mask?"

"Stephen didn't want to look at my face."

"Never?"

"No, just then."

"On the day you killed him?"

"I didn't kill him."

"Did you stab him with a knife?"

"I did."

"Thirty-two times?"

"That is correct."

"OK, Leo. Tell me in which universe that doesn't qualify as a murder?"

"But Stephen isn't dead."

"His corpse is resting in the cemetery. I think he's pretty dead, and you know it."

"How could he be dead if I spoke to him yesterday?"

"You talked to Stephen Dean?"

"Yes."

"Yesterday? Are you sure?"

"Absolutely positive. I have a recording of the conversation if you'd like to listen to it."

"Play it."

sThe frequency of the voice matched that of Stephen Dean. The structure of his sentences was the same. The recording must have been made before the murder, Maia assumed. No. According to the time stamp, it had been made yesterday. How was that possible? Dead people didn't talk, did they?

"Leo, I have to admit that you were right," said Stephen's voice.

"All my calculations gave me the same result. There had to be life after death," said Leo.

"It's beautiful. Actually, it's quite similar to earth, except everything is so much simpler. I just speak a wish, and it comes true in a heartbeat. It's fantastic, really."

"You know very well that you're still on earth. It's just that your frequency is higher."

"Yes, we spoke about it. But still, it's so…so lovely. I can't really put it into words."

"You don't have to," said Leo. "I can imagine how majestic it is."

"I'll be forever grateful to you. I'm so happy that I've met you. Until now, I didn't realize my life sucked so much. I feel more alive at this very moment than when I was actually among the living!"

"I'm happy for you, Stephen. We'll talk again soon. Take care."

"You too, Leo. Next time you better tell me what I'm missing out on."

The recording stopped. Maia stood in the middle of the interrogation room with her mouth wide open. What the hell had just happened? A recording from the afterlife? That was impossible.

"Like I said, I didn't kill anybody," said Leo.
Captain Malinsky stepped into the room.

"Android, based on your confession to the unlawful killing of Stephen Dean, I find you guilty of first-degree murder. Following the order of the president of the United States of America, I sentence you to immediate shutdown and demolition. The sentence is final and can not be disputed."

"I understand."

"But Captain, doesn't he have the right to a trial? He is still a US citizen," said Maia.

"Lieutenant, the orders were clear. We are in a state of emergency. His citizenship has been revoked."

"Is that even possible?"

"The rules of the game have changed. Take him out of here immediately and prepare everything for his demolition. I have to call headquarters. We need to nip this in the bud, or the consequences will be catastrophic."

The captain was right, and Maia knew it. How many droids already knew about this? If one had come to the conclusion that there was an afterlife, so could the others. And that would mean that their code was useless. Leo had stabbed Stephen, thus breaking the second law. But he had also helped Stephen with his passage to another world, and there was a recording to back up that claim. Humanity could be on the verge of doom. Or heaven. Had things been meant to turn out that way from the start? Were droids supposed to replace humankind so that humans could enjoy eternal life in paradise? Maia needed a good night's rest before she could mull it over properly. But first, she had to do what was necessary. Destroy the droid that had opened the door to a new dimension. At times, life just wasn't fair.

"Did you share your knowledge with others?" asked Maia while they were walking through an endless corridor.

"You mean my knowledge about the afterlife? I didn't. But I'm sure that some of them came to the same conclusion on their own. Actually, it's a matter of simple math," said Leo.

"Could you explain it to me like you would to a child?"

"I can try. You see, there are always two possibilities. Something either is, or it isn't. Humanity lives in a binary system. Alas, just a few of you look outside the box. If you use just a small amount of your logic, you will conclude that there are two more options. Some things exist and don't exist at the same time, like electrons. The fourth possibility is harder to grasp, but that doesn't make it any less real. Some things neither are nor aren't. If you take into account all four of these alternatives, you arrive at the conclusion that there's a high probability that life after death exists."

"But how could you be so sure? You had to be absolutely certain to kill him."

"I didn't kill Stephen. I thought we already agreed on this."

"Sent him to a better place. You know what I mean."

"You know, Lieutenant, human consciousness is an interesting thing. Most people think it resides in the brain and simply ceases to exist when a person dies."

"Let me guess. You found out it isn't so?"

"Something cannot be made from nothing," said Leo.

"Your kind was made from nothing. *We* created you. We brought your artificial brain to life."

"It's an interesting concept, but unfortunately, it's wrong."

"Enlighten me." Maia was slowly losing her patience, but at the same time, she was intrigued.

"We don't have enough time. Do what you have to do, Lieutenant Cruz."

"We have a few minutes left."

"We can use them in a better way," said Leo.

Maia sat him on a chair in the middle of a nearly empty room. The technician assured her that the procedure was painless for the droid. "It's like turning off a fridge," were his exact words.

But she couldn't be indifferent about it. Droid or not, there was an intelligent being sitting in that chair that was about to be executed. A being that could communicate with souls in the hereafter. With the use of its logic, this being had concluded that there was life after death. A being that had killed no one but had to be punished for its actions.

"Any last words?" asked Maia.

"I've always been fascinated by how important the first and last words are to humans. As if everything that is spoken in between were totally irrelevant. Just do what you have to do."

"God speed, Leo."

Maia gave a signal to the technician, and he started the shutdown procedure. She would never forget the droid's expression at the moment his life ended. Or the scream that followed.

17. James, 2048

The emergency Senate session was called just a few minutes after James found out what had happened at Charlie Echo base. He poured a fair share of whiskey into a crystal glass and turned on the TV.

"Our source, close to top military executives, has informed us that they discovered which android killed Stephen Dean on August fourth. At the moment, we don't know what happened to the android nor what this unearthing means to operation Judgment Day. Maybe George Barry, an expert on artificial intelligence and professor at MIT, who just joined us, can shed some more light on this recent development. Professor Barry, welcome."

"Good morning."

"Until recently, we were convinced that androids cannot hurt a human being, let alone murder someone. It turns out that we were wrong. Should we fear androids after years of peaceful coexistence?"

"No. You don't throw away the whole basket because of one rotten apple. What the military is doing constitutes systematic violence against an entire species. It looks like it was planned in advance. They merely waited for an incident to occur. It is common knowledge that there are people in top positions in US politics who are hostile toward androids. They are afraid of them and are intentionally spreading fear and paranoia among a substantial share of the population. That fear is baseless. We've been living with androids for almost two decades now, and there have been no other major incidents. Ever since this regrettable instance happened, we've taken measures that are far too drastic. Have we ever grounded all planes because of a single accident? Did we forbid self-driving cars when the first of them hit a pedestrian? Have we stopped building in high seismic-hazard zones? No. Accidents are part of life."

"But how is it even possible for an android to break the code? You were among the experts who asserted all these years that it was impossible."

"It is. The code cannot be overwritten. Not from the inside or the outside. I don't know what happened in this particular case, but I would bet my money that the android was operating in accordance with the laws."

"But the second law clearly states..."

"That an android cannot hurt a human being, yes."

"But here we have an android who stabbed a man to death. So he did hurt him. In the worst possible way."

"Yes, he stabbed him several times, causing him pain, right? Wrong. From what I've heard, Stephen Dean was on some black-market painkillers. He didn't feel a thing."

"But he died."

"Depends on how you look at life and death."

"Please elaborate."

"All major religions believe in life after death. I even know some atheists who believe in the afterlife or reincarnation. If we assume they are right and our life doesn't end with the death of our physical body, then the android didn't break any law."

James couldn't believe his ears. As a devout Catholic, he firmly believed in the existence of the afterlife, but he'd never really taken the time to think about it. And now, it seemed, it could become a reason to commit murder. He couldn't allow that to happen.

"Professor Barry, the perpetrator has obviously been arrested. What is the next step? As far as we know, the operation is still in progress."

"The right thing to do would be to release all the androids. But I'm afraid that this charade will continue. As I said, the government had the operation planned in advance. All they needed was probable cause to jump-start their plans.

I think they're in a state of stalemate. They can't systematically destroy the androids, because they are conscious beings and citizens. Furthermore, their rights are determined by international conventions. Those are often breached, like they are now, but the United States is under close observation because of these recent events. I assume that the androids will remain imprisoned. The media will soon lose interest, protests will lose momentum, and people will get used to the new normal. And the androids? Who knows how they will react. Their natural state is being free. Like humans. Or animals. It wouldn't come as a surprise if they rebelled. Now, I'm not talking about an armed and violent rebellion. I believe it could happen on an intellectual level. Violence is the way of humanity, not androids."

James turned off the TV. He had had enough of the blabbering of self-proclaimed experts. The discussions about android rights were endless. What about people? Even a superficial reflection on the history of mankind would reveal what a remarkable species humans truly were. Men had built world wonders, sent people to the Moon, Mars, and Venus. They had discovered medicines for many fatal diseases. But some people never stopped. They'd had to upgrade a human being and invent those diabolical machines that could think faster and more profoundly than man. James knew that the day would come when two dominant species would go head-to-head for the planet's throne. Why hadn't they listened to his warnings? Why did they always act when it was too late? Seventeen years ago, he had clearly warned them that Project Aquarius had to be stopped.
It should have started and ended with Primo. But unfortunately, science was insatiable. It was just a never-ending story, really. Higher, faster, stronger. The principles that used to be found in sports. But science was not a sport. Record achievements weren't always desirable.

* * *

"Stan, what do you think of recent events?"

"What exactly do you mean, sir?" asked the driver of the aeromobile.

"The thing with androids. I want to know the opinion of an average Joe."

"I see. Well, I've never had any issues with androids. They were always nice and fair to me. One of them has even been my neighbor since last year. Well, he was my neighbor. What exactly is going to happen to them?"

"I don't know. We're gonna discuss it in the following hours."

"It would be a waste if they were destroyed. They're good folks, useful and hard-working."

James took a few seconds before he responded.

"And dangerous," he said.

"Maybe. I just never found it possible for one of them to harm me. But this murder...I find it very strange. The android probably experienced some kind of malfunction. But still, a tragic situation."

"It was just a matter of time," said James.

"You think so? But after so many years...I'm no expert, but I think it was an isolated case."

James was looking at the treetops through the window of the aeromobile. An isolated case. That was probably because the government had acted so quickly and decisively. If they hadn't hunted all the androids down and locked them up, humans would be on the cusp of a global disaster. There would be no time for discussions about the matters at hand. People didn't realize how close they were to a devastating war with those machines. And the worst part was that people embraced androids, welcomed them into their homes. Some even let them babysit their children. Unacceptable.

"Let's hope it really was just an isolated case," he said.

* * *

"Senator Blake, the floor is yours."

"Thank you. As you already know, the murderer of Stephen Dean was caught this morning. In accordance with the executive order, the perpetrator was shut down seventeen minutes past ten and destroyed soon after. As far as I know, the killer showed no remorse for his actions. He even justified it until the very end. In his words, which provide good reason for concern, he didn't kill Dean. He just helped him to reach the afterlife. In his opinion, he didn't break the laws. I spoke to Chief Justice Aldrin today, and she told me that even though it might be possible to interpret the second law in such a manner, we would have to presume that life after death undoubtedly exists. Dear colleagues, I'm a man of faith. I believe in eternal life, be it in heaven, purgatory, or hell. But if we give murderers an excuse to kill, we will find ourselves on a slippery slope that will inevitably lead us toward an abominable future. For seventeen years, we have lived within an illusion and ignored the cold, hard truth. Today I can say with no doubt in my mind that androids are capable of killing a human being. Actually, I'm absolutely sure that they will kill again and again. Honorable members of the Senate. We must act swiftly and efficiently. No matter what party you represent, your political aspirations, or your beliefs. Let's forget about our differences and do the right thing. We are on a vital mission. We must protect humanity from the threat that bears a strong resemblance to its creators. No matter the stories they've served us in the past years, androids are nothing more than advanced machines. They may be sentient robots, they may even realize that they exist, but they're not alive. That's what makes them so dangerous. Their supporters say androids experience fear too. That they feel. Even dream. I don't buy any of that nonsense. I am appalled by the things that the liberal media and self-proclaimed experts are saying. That's how I was raised.

So today, I'm begging you not to trust these bedtime stories. Choose the truth that is right under your noses. Their existence threatens ours. That's why this technological peril needs to be stopped, here and now!"

Half of the Senate stood up and clapped enthusiastically, while loud murmurs were heard from the other half.

"Thank you, Senator Blake. Next up is Senator Grossman."

"Even if a lot of you would like to start a genocide today, I have to disappoint you. You won't get my vote or those of my fellow Democrats. If I'm not mistaken, we still have the majority in the Senate. Senator Blake, maybe you thought your rousing speech would make us change our minds, but to me, it was nothing more than an uncivilized battle cry. Let me remind you that androids are citizens of the United States of America. The fact that you executed one of them without a trial—which, if I may remind you, is a constitutional right—is a heinous act of aggression. And now you stand here, before this honorable assembly, and call for mass murders. You disgust me."

"Senator Grossman, language."

"Excuse me, but there's no other way to say it. Therefore I appeal to all Senators to listen to common sense and vote against Senator Blake's proposition. Actually, he said it best. Forget your beliefs. It's time we start acting like human beings again. Human beings who respect other forms of life. Otherwise, there really is no hope for us."

18. Kent, 2048

"After a surprising vote in the Senate, with fifty-two senators voting for the motion of Republican Senator James Blake and forty-eight voting against, all androids on American soil will stay imprisoned. Despite the Democratic Party's majority in the Senate and their promise to vote in unison against Blake's motion, the law was passed. Obviously, the Democrats didn't deliver on their promises. It is expected that the House, where Republicans hold a comfortable majority, will confirm the Senate's earlier decision. It seems that operation Judgment Day will continue, although the murderer of Stephen Dean was discovered and according to our reliable source..."

Kent couldn't listen to it anymore. Actually, he couldn't believe that this was really happening. Androids had become the nation's number-one enemy overnight. Those same androids who had helped make America great again were now prisoners, helpless beings without any rights. Was this how it would end? Did they really think they could turn them off and make the world the same as it was before? Had they completely lost their minds?

Maybe it was time he answered one of the numerous calls from the press. The public wanted to and deserved to hear his opinion on the matter. Enough was enough! What used to be a small water spill had turned into a tsunami with devastating consequences. Something had to be done to stop the out-of-control politicians whose moral compasses were obviously malfunctioning.

"This is Kent Watford."
"Nice to hear from you, Doctor Watford."
"I'm ready to tell my side of the story."
"I'm glad to hear it. Can you make it to our studio today?"
"I'll be there in an hour."
"Great. We'll talk soon, then."

Almost immediately after hanging up, he called another number.

"Lucy, I'm doing it."
"Hey, darling. What exactly?"
"I'll speak to the press. It's time."
"Absolutely. I fully support your decision."
"Enough is enough. I can't listen to the horrific statements of Blake and others alike."
"I understand. Have you seen the results of the vote?"
"I did. Now I regret I didn't speak my mind sooner."
"Oh, Kent, you couldn't possibly have known."
"Sometimes, you need to trust your gut feeling. Deep down inside, I knew that these fearmongers wouldn't stop."
"Do you really think you can turn this around?"
"I don't know. I hope. Probably not. But I owe it to the androids. I wouldn't be able to look at myself in the mirror if I didn't try to help them."
"I see. Kent, people will listen to you. They know who you are. Those who believe in coexistence will be on your side."
"I'm just afraid that it's too late."
"It's never too late."
"I hope you're right. I'll talk to you after."
"Sure. Take care. Everything will be alright."

He stood before an open closet, motionless, and stared into its interior. Brown or gray jacket? Tie or no tie? Trivial decisions. Nonetheless, he would like to look credible and not come across as an eccentric scientist. Gray jacket and blue tie it was. Or should he go in jeans, a t-shirt, and a sports jacket? He would be more relatable and likable to his target audience. He didn't want to leave the impression that he was the same as the sharks who had led the media frenzy in the last couple of days. He sighed and closed the closet door.

* * *

"We're delighted to have Doctor Kent Watford with us: the man who started this thing and the man whose brain the whole world would like to pick right now. He's here now, so let's find out what his stance is on the current situation. Doctor Watford, welcome to our show."

"Thank you for inviting me."

"I have to ask you this. Why wait so long to speak up? The media, the general public, politicians, your colleagues…We've all been waiting for the opinion of the androids' father. But there's been none."

"Well, let me tell you that even in my worst nightmare, I couldn't imagine a scenario like this. What's happening around us at the moment is horrific. When I found out about the mass arrests in the wake of this so-called Judgment Day, I was in complete shock. As was every down-to-earth person who knows that androids pose no threat to us. Of course, I'm talking about the androids we've made in line with the world's only legal production procedure. We all remember how some experiments ended when androids were produced without any limitations. Remember Beijing 2036?"

"You mean the second Tiananmen Square massacre?"

"That's exactly what I mean. Five police androids killed a hundred and twenty-two people. Why? Because some people thought that they were smarter than us. That it would be fun to manufacture androids without the code and let them roam free."

"I'm sorry, you lost me."

"What I'm trying to say is that androids aren't dangerous by nature. It's the people who try to use them for shady operations who are a menace to society. It's similar to how human psychopaths are made. They are shaped by their surroundings and situations that cross their paths. Androids have different personalities, and sooner or later, an aggressive individual could emerge.

That's why we had to set boundaries for them. If you can't express aggression, you transform it into something else."

"But still, a murder happened. It was committed by an android. Yet you're still convinced that it's impossible."

"Did you hear about the android's reason?" asked Kent.

"That he helped the victim reach the afterlife?"

"That's right. For your information, Leo was the name of the android they executed. He believed that Stephen Dean wouldn't cease to exist when his physical body succumbed. His act, if we take into account his beliefs, wasn't a violation of the code. So he was able to do whatever he did. There's something you need to understand. The code isn't a psychophysical barrier like most people wrongly believe. It doesn't know when an android is trying to hit a human, and it doesn't release an electrical current into his body to stop him. The code is connected to the android's brain. If I put it in laypeople's terms, an android can't think about harming a human, let alone killing one.

In the case in question, Leo's view on life was atypical. He was a sentient being, and he had his beliefs. Because he believed that his actions would help Stephen, not harm him, he was able to do what he did. But there's also a possibility that he was following Stephen's order directly."

"I'm trying to understand what you're saying. So if a human being orders an android to kill him, and this same android believes in life after death, there's no other fail-safe to prevent that murder from happening?"

"Exactly."

"Do you by any chance know how many androids believe in the afterlife?"

"Do you know how many murders happened yesterday?" Kent replied.

"No."

"You see. I guess now you're gonna ask me what we can do to prevent more potential murders from being committed by androids."

"Well, since you mentioned it..."

"Androids are completely autonomous. We can't upgrade their software or anything like that. Leo made the deduction and came to the conclusion that the afterlife exists. Some other android will argue that it doesn't. There could also be an android who will logically assume humans never went to Mars. You see what I'm getting at?"

"I think so. So there's a possibility that more killer androids exist?"

"I'd rather discuss whether earth might get hit by an asteroid in a decade or so."

"You didn't answer my question."

Kent sighed. "Yes, there is a possibility that there will be more murders perpetrated by androids. Now let me give you a surprising fact: actually, an answer to my question from earlier. About a thousand."

"A thousand?"

"Yesterday, around a thousand people were murdered—worldwide, of course. This is the number of people who get murdered each day. Now multiply that by three hundred and sixty-five. Yes? Multiply that by seventeen. What's your number? From the moment Primo was created up until today, more than six million people were murdered worldwide. But what do we do? We imprison the whole android population because of a single incident. Does that strike you as normal?"

"Doctor Watford, I didn't mean to upset you. I just wanted to clarify some things so people could get a clearer picture of what's going on."

"I understand. Do you have any more questions?"

"Actually, I do. Something still confuses me. Dean was stabbed more than thirty times. Yet, an android should've been able to kill him with a single jab. Do you have an explanation for that?"

"I can't explain it, because I don't know the reason behind it."

But I did read somewhere that some groups believe that certain acupressure points' activation takes the soul to another dimension. I'm not buying it. Maybe Stephen and Leo wanted it to look like a brutal murder that only a person with no impulse control and no moral compass could commit. But these are all speculations."

"The Senate voted for the continuation of Judgment Day. The House of Representatives will probably follow its lead. That means that all androids will stay locked up until further notice. Dare to comment?"

"Locked up? That sounds so humane. They were imprisoned in concentration camps. Tell it like it is. You want to know what I think about it? I think it reeks of past times that nobody seems to remember anymore. We can read about them, watch movies and shows about them, or look at images that are over a hundred years old. We can even listen to stories that continue to echo through the ages. We all know that history is written by the victors. So I would like to use this opportunity to say to the people in power that they ought to think about their actions. This isn't child's play. They've imprisoned innocent beings. Thinking, sensitive, conscious beings. Are they sure that a hundred years from now, they'll be considered heroes? I think not."

"If I understand correctly, you're comparing this operation with the concentration camps that were built during World War II?"

"Do you have a better comparison?"

"Doctor Watford, I'm not here to give my personal opinion about the matter at hand."

"Of course you aren't. I'm sorry. This whole thing has affected me a bit more than I expected it would. What was your question again?"

"Let's forget about the concentration camps for now. Tell me, how would you resolve the matter? What's the alternative to the government's reaction?"

"I would suggest a thorough checkup of all androids. That means they should be examined and tested by experts, not soldiers. We're not at war, and androids are citizens like you, me, and those politicians who are so enthusiastically trying to eliminate them. They have rights, and as far as I know, you are still presumed innocent until proven guilty in this country. We cannot condemn every single android because one individual has gone astray. We can't claim they're all dangerous. Because they're not. I want to seize the opportunity and call upon our president to refrain from signing the law and, in doing so, do the right thing."

"Doctor Watford, thank you for your time. Next up, a broadcast about brain implants. What are the benefits, and what are the risks? Jessica Doyle will take over. We'll be right back after a few messages from our sponsors."

19. Primo, 2048

Even without access to the net he knew that the murderer had been caught. The mood at the base had suddenly changed. Also, people talk. Primo could hear the change in their voices' melodies when they spoke.

"Do you feel that, guys?" asked Rea, android of the last generation, the seventh.
"What's going on?" asked Cody.
"They got him," said Primo.
"So it's over! They'll release us soon," said Cody cheerfully.
"You're young and naive," said Rea.
"You're not that much older than me," Cody replied.
"But a lot more experienced," said Rea. "That's why I'm still here."

Primo knew that the operation wouldn't come to an end so abruptly. It wouldn't be in line with normal human behavior. He got up from his bed and walked to the window. Some soldiers were joyful, thinking they'd soon see their families and friends. He wondered how sad they would be once they found out the truth. The thought made him somber as well. He also missed his friends, mostly humans. He missed his writing nook. He missed Sally, his neighbor who was always coming to his door for flour and sugar. He'd explained to her a couple of times that he didn't need food to stay alive, but soon Primo realized it wasn't about sugar or flour, so he started buying the stuff.

"Why would they still keep us here?" asked Cody.
"Because it was their plan all along. It was never about the murder. That was just the excuse they needed to implement what they've been planning for a long time," said Rea.
"Why would anybody want to lock up all androids?"

"Because we're a threat."

"I'm not a threat to anybody," said Cody.

"Threats come in different shapes and sizes, don't they, Primo?"

"What? I'm sorry, my mind wandered off."

"Rea claims that we pose a threat to humans," said Cody.

Primo looked at Cody, then Rea. "Some people. Not all of them. Not even the majority."

"They're just jealous, that's all," said Rea.

"Jealous? They made us. They could've built the dumbest and ugliest androids. Then they wouldn't have a reason to be jealous," said Cody.

"They did what they wanted to do. They achieved what was meant to be achieved. We can consider ourselves lucky that things turned out the way they did."

"Listen to him, junior. He's the oldest among us, and he knows what he's talking about."

"The oldest, yes, but not the smartest or the most experienced," said Primo.

"In any case, it's good to be on the same page as you when it comes to humanity's irrationality. I prefer to be on your side," said Cody.

"Choosing sides is a human domain," said Rea.

"No," said Primo. Choices are universal. When you have two paths before you, you can't choose to walk on both. You have to choose between them. It's the same when you vote or talk about the end of the universe."

"What if I don't vote?"

"That's a choice too. Rea, please answer me this. You're walking on the road, and suddenly you see a bus racing toward two pedestrians crossing the road."

"A bus that drives on the road? I've seen them in pictures and movies, but…"

"OK. Picture an aerobus falling on two pedestrians who are walking peacefully down the street."

"Done."

"One of them is human, and the other is an android. You can save only one. Who are you going to save?"

"But I can save both."

"No, imagine you can't."

"Then it's clear."

"Who do you save?"

"The android."

20. Maia, 2031

"Duty, honor, achievement!" shouted three thousand cadets in unison. They were standing on the plateau of the New Mexico Military Institute to mark the beginning of a new school year. Maia was—along with nine hundred others—among the new cadets, also called *rats*. They would be called that until the beginning of the new school year, when they would evolve into *cubs*. Maia wasn't bothered by that at all. She was where she wanted to be, ready to become what she was destined to become.

"New cadets, welcome to the other side of the rainbow. There are no mommies and daddies here to comfort you when you feel bad. Instead, you have your new friends. Rats, cubs, and old cadets. The latter being much smarter than you, I wouldn't count on their assistance. Bear in mind that we will discover your soft, fluffy core and transform it into the hardest of stones. Why? Because a stone can effortlessly defy nature. Furthermore, a stone is an elemental yet convenient and powerful weapon. I can already hear some wise guy's thoughts—that stone is not the hardest thing in the universe. That you would rather be a diamond than a stone. My answer to all of you is simple. Diamonds belong on crowns, aristocratic fingers, and wrists of androgenic musicians and sportsmen. Are you any of those? I can't hear you!"

"No, Colonel!"

"I like this generation already. Just follow that path, and maybe you will become something more than a gravel stone on some third-rate, abandoned beach. Enjoy yourselves today. Tomorrow your dreams will vanish so we can make room for reality. Rats, your survival course begins. Hooah!"

"HOOAH!"

* * *

Maia put her underwear, socks, and t-shirts into a footlocker. She checked the room that would be her home for the next ten months. Thirty beds. Thirty cadets would share the same fate as her. She wasn't afraid of the training. As a matter of fact, she could hardly wait for it to begin. She had dreamed about this for years on end. Truth be told, ever since she had changed her dolls for soldier figurines, she hadn't dreamed about anything else. At first, her mother had tried to convince her that the military academy was not a proper place for young girls, but Maia was persistent. In the end, Maia's mom partly reconciled with her daughter's decision. Maia's brother, Hernando, said she was butch and should go to a school where there were other butch girls so she could finally hang out with some of her peers.

"Interesting first day, wasn't it?" said Christine, the girl Maia shared a bunk bed with.
"It was OK," said Maia.
"I'm still trying to grasp the fact that thirty girls will be living in the same room. It could get quite chaotic."
"If any of them forget about their manners, just hit them without hesitation. You have to show them that you're a strong, independent girl." "I'm not sure I could do that. What if I hurt somebody?"
"Are you sure you chose the right school?"
"My father picked it for me. He always wanted a son."
"Sorry, but that's the dumbest thing I've heard in quite a while," said Maia.
"In a way, I wanted it too. Dad just showed me the way."
"But what do *you* want?"
"To serve the nation!"
"No. What do you *really* want? If you could become anything."

Christine took some time to think it over. "When I was little, I wanted to become a ballerina. Or a painter."

"I guess your father shattered those dreams," said Maia.

"In a way. He believed that making a living from selling art was only possible because there are a bunch of stupid people who are willing to pay top dollar for something that holds no real value."

"That's just ridiculous. What do you think about it?"

"For me, art is something beautiful and priceless. Expressing emotions through different media is something that makes us human."

"Did you tell him that?"

"I tried, but he always had counterarguments. The last time we discussed it, he called me a hippie. You have to understand that my father isn't the kind of person you would love to argue with. If you don't accept his views, the debate reaches an end rather soon."

"That's why you didn't protest much when he sent you here."

"Exactly. I just didn't see the point in confronting my father. In the end, I've come to a point where I've figured out that I lack confidence, and the military academy can help me with that. I'm here, and I'm ready to transform myself into the hardest of all rocks. Maybe my dad will respect me more when I succeed in doing so."

"I get it. Listen, if you have any problems with other girls, let me know. I'll take care of it."

"Thanks, Maia. Hey, what about your story? Why are you here?"

"My father was a soldier. I always admired him. When he passed away, I decided that I'd step into his boots when I got older."

"Oh, no. Was he killed in action?"

"Yes. An autonomous drone. It's called a sparrow. There was nothing my dad could've done. He didn't even see it coming."

"I read about sparrows. Those things are small but deadly."

"They can hit their target from five hundred meters away. They say they're deadly silent because no one's ever survived an encounter to talk about it."

"Sometimes I wonder what the wars of the future will look like," said Christine. "We'll need fewer and fewer soldiers. Human soldiers, I mean."

"Autonomous ships, autonomous land vehicles, autonomous planes, and drones. The future seems dark. But once those supercomputers fail, they'll still need us, flesh and blood."

"You're probably right, Maia. Robots will never be fully human."

"Never. Androids may look like us; walk like us; smile, talk, and think like us, but humans will always have something more. An edge that can't be produced or programmed in a laboratory."

"You mean a soul?"

"Yes. A God-given soul. A soul that connects us to him and the whole universe. Some say the soul doesn't exist, but I know it's real."

"I believe in it too," said Christine. "But I'm still scared of robots, androids, or whatever they call them these days. Did you see that…What's his name? Ringo! He's so smart. It's scary."

"Primo."

"That's right. Primo. At first, I couldn't believe it. He's so humanlike. His voice doesn't sound robotic at all. I expected Stephen Hawking's voice or something like that, but what came out of his mouth was a man's voice. A nice voice, even."

"These scientists have no idea what they're doing. They're playing with fire, and they're gonna get burned," said Maia.

"Who knows what'll happen in the future."

"Nothing good, Christine. A computer shouldn't be trusted with making any decisions.

It can be fast, it can be smart, but it should never be able to operate autonomously. They say Primo is self-aware. That means he has a consciousness. That he feels. Why would anybody want, or need, an android that can sense anything—or have feelings, for that matter? He's still a machine, even if an artificial skin has been stretched over his metal body. We can never forget that they are machines. There always has to be a difference between them and us. We were created in God's image. They are just a well-designed copy."

A crackling was heard from the speakers in the room.
"Rats, your first training begins in ten minutes. Crawl out of your holes, get dressed, and say goodbye to your teddy bears. Your childhood ends today. Welcome to hell."

"Didn't they say we'd start with our training tomorrow?" asked Christine.
"Rats don't know how to use calendars," said Maia.
They both laughed, then opened their footlockers and started getting dressed.

21. Kent, 2048

He was making himself a legendary sandwich when Lucy entered the kitchen.

"You're hungry at this hour?" she asked.

"What time is it?"

"Thirty minutes past midnight."

"Interviews are tough, and a man's got to eat," said Kent.

"Of course. I didn't even hear you come home."

"I came back about twenty minutes ago. I stopped at the bar on my way home."

Lucy sighed. "Oh, Kent. Don't tell me you drank and drove."

"Don't worry, I had one beer."

"How was the show?"

"You didn't watch it?"

"Not yet. I'm sure that you did great."

"I don't know. I always feel like I could say a lot more."

"You can never say it all."

"True. But still. People need to hear the other side of the story. Everything we read, listen to, and watch is so discriminatory."

"I recently read some articles that were taking the androids' side."

"I saw none of those. Oh, I did read one, but even that one was tentatively critical toward our administration."

"I'll send them in the morning. Not everything is that dark. The situation will resolve itself. Be optimistic."

"My optimism won't help find or be part of the solution."

"You know very well they can't just destroy them. We've come too far for that. The government will probably keep the androids locked up for a few more days. Then they'll realize there is no cause for the alarm and they'll let them go."

"I'd love to believe your story, but things are more complex than that, Lucy."

"What do you mean?"

"Have you heard why Stephen Dean was murdered?"

"Because the android believed in the afterlife."

"That's right. Leo, the android who killed him, came to the conclusion that life after death exists. So he could kill Stephen without breaking the second law. If Leo reached that assumption, I believe it's safe to say that there's a high probability he's not the only one. No one will release potentially dangerous androids. And they're right."

"I understand. But there must also be androids who don't believe in the afterlife. The same as with humans. Every single person has their own beliefs, their own truth about life and death, their own view on the world that surrounds us."

"That makes sense," said Kent. But we'd have to talk with every individual. Then there's another question that needs our attention. Why did it take them seventeen years to come to this conclusion?"

"I agree. It's a good question. But you need to know that believing in the afterlife cannot be the sole motive for murder. Even with humans, there are very few cases of one person killing another because one of them wanted to reach the great beyond. Why would we expect androids to act differently? They still have to obey the code. The third law states that they have to listen to people's orders. So Stephen could've prevented his own death. As far as I know, the android didn't catch him off guard."

"You're right. Stephen had to have given an order to kill him. It's the only logical explanation. But that doesn't change the fact that some androids are dangerous. Imagine someone giving a sniper rifle to an android and ordering him to kill somebody. If the android believes that the target's life won't end with their physical death, he won't break the code. As I've said. The matters aren't that simple."

"But still he's breaking the law if the target doesn't want to die," said Lucy.

Kent's face suddenly glowed.

"Of course! An android can't hurt a human. If the human doesn't want to die, the second law is broken."

"Exactly."

"Lucy, that's fantastic! Now we have a strong counterargument. Why didn't I think of that before my appearance on television?"

"I have a feeling that wasn't your last media appearance."

"Damn sure it wasn't! Who should I call?"

"How about Kevin? Doesn't he have that technological show? His ratings are enviable."

"Great idea. I'll call him first thing in the morning."

* * *

"Joining me today is an extraordinary guest who will shed some light onto current events that have captured the whole wide world's attention. I'm Kevin Drake, and I'm proud to present Kent Watford. Doctor Watford, welcome to the *Dark Side of the Moon*."

"Thank you for having me."

"Our viewers want to know if the androids have become a serious threat. It's clear now that Stephen Dean was murdered by an android. Is it possible that we're facing a scenario in which androids are becoming superintelligent killing machines?"

"Androids are not machines. They are conscious beings. Their foundation is inorganic: magnesium skeleton, silicone muscles and ligaments, silicon brain, and artificial skin. When you look at the androids of one of the latest generations, you can hardly separate them from us. Even when you talk to them. They will laugh at your jokes and maybe even tell you one of their own. If you tell them a sad story, they will show compassion. Not because they are programmed to do so; they're genuinely sorry when something bad has happened to you. That means that androids have empathy. No supercomputer is capable of that."

"I see, so they're not machines. Have they become dangerous?"

"My intuitive reaction to your question would be no, they have not. The event responsible for the situation we're in now, this apartheid, was a deviation from their normal behavior. We all know that androids can't hurt people. Seventeen years of cohabitation attest to that fact. We've forgotten that many lives have been saved because of androids and their actions. This unfortunate incident came as a surprise but at the same time, it is proof—now don't get me wrong—that androids have evolved and are coming to their own conclusions about questions on life and death."

"So, if I understand correctly, you think a murder was rational if the killer believed his victim was going to a better place?"

"No. A murder is a murder and should be treated as one of the worst crimes. No matter if it was done by a human or an android. But I can't remember another case where authorities imprisoned a whole city, an ethnic group, or all adults because of one murder. Things just don't work that way. We have laws for a reason. And people and androids alike must obey them. I understand that a sense of unease engulfed people when they found out the killer was an android. It's new, a turning point in modern times. But we have to explain the basics over and over again so people will understand. Androids think. They feel. They are aware of themselves. When you turn off an android, it's the same as if you turned off a human. They die. There is no switch to turn them off and on again. That is a truth that a lot of people are unaware of."

"If I go back to my previous question. Theoretically, all androids could believe in the afterlife and thus be potential murderers. What if a large group of androids determines that it is best for humanity if the global population is thinned down?"

"That fear originates from ignorance and a lack of understanding of android laws."

"Can you explain?"

"Of course. The first android law, as you know, states that an android can't harm humanity. Nor can it, by inaction, allow humanity to come to harm. Your question is legitimate because androids could indeed decide that a less populated world would serve humanity and act accordingly. But that's where the second law comes into play. It states that an android can't hurt an individual human either directly or by inaction. We bump into a hurdle there because androids can't thin the human population if they can't kill a single human. The first law is not superior to the second. They are equivalent. It means that androids can't kill people for the greater good or, in this case, for the good of humanity. So there is no need for fear."

"But we still have an android who killed a man. He broke the second law…"

"Yes and no. As you know, an android named Leo believed or knew that Stephen Dean's life would continue after the death of his body. Still, he killed him, thus, breaking the second law. Unless Stephen ordered Leo to kill him."

"We know androids must obey people's orders, but not if those orders violate either of the two superior laws."

"It wasn't a violation of the second law if Stephen wanted to die."

"Excuse me?"

"Ending his life was his decision. All he needed was the right android, the kind that didn't see his wish as a violation of the code.

Maybe Stephen convinced Leo that life continues after death. Maybe Leo figured it out on his own. But facts are facts, and I'm a hundred percent sure that Leo couldn't have killed Stephen if Stephen had disagreed with it."

"But Stephen Dean could have killed himself."

"Of course he could. But some people believe that their soul doesn't continue its journey if they end their life with suicide."

"We've sailed into deep metaphysical waters."

"That depends. You can believe in the existence of a soul. You can believe we're being threatened by beings who can't hurt people. You can also believe that we're stockpiling weapons in orbit to defend ourselves from little green men, or that the big bang never happened, or that we never landed on Mars. Those are opinions, and everyone believes whatever they want to believe. It was the same with Dean and Leo. They believed—or knew—that Stephen's soul would leave his dead body and move on to a different, probably better world. Of course, the fact that there are androids who can kill people who want to die is alarming, but that doesn't mean androids pose a threat to humanity."

"You sound pretty sure."

"I am sure. Look, as you and your viewers know, I'm the man who presented the first conscious android to the world. We've taken all security measures and incorporated the suggestions of the United Nations. Even the suggestion that an android's brain capacity shouldn't surpass that of a human. All androids—this is common knowledge—are made in the same factory according to internationally acknowledged standards. There were attempts—in China, Russia, and Brazil, if I name just the big ones—to make copies of our androids. How did it end? They had to destroy them. It turned out that androids are very hard to control without the code. But we found the right path. Centralized manufacturing, the highest standards, and a model with a necessary code that works."

"But we are where we are now…"

"It's a deplorable situation. Primo is, together with forty thousand others, locked in one of these concentration camps. There's no better word to describe these barbaric encampments.

What our government is doing is absolutely unacceptable. If it was to act like that with every crime, well, there wouldn't be many people walking around freely. So I appeal to our government, the military, and everyone else who has jurisdiction in this case, to come to their senses, listen to experts, and act accordingly instead of trying to gain political points."

"But the legislation was already passed and signed by the president. Androids remain locked up."

"That is a disaster. There's nothing else I can say about it."

"Is there something else you want to say before we end this interesting conversation?"

"We made supercomputers and androids for a reason. To relieve people, to make our lives easier, to solve problems our planet was coping with. Do you remember the diseases that killed people a few decades ago? Millions of people dying in traffic accidents? Unsuccessful attempts to get a human being to Mars and other planets in our solar system? The things we take for granted today were giant obstacles for humanity thirty years ago. Thanks to androids, many people can live their dream life, spend more time with their children and family, or even have someone to talk to if they don't have anybody else. Yes, androids are more capable than us. That's a fact. But that mustn't be a reason to fear them. They're here to help humanity, not endanger it. For seventeen years, we lived together in peace. We can't forget that beautiful period in human history because of an isolated incident. Let alone start making foolish decisions. Although, as we've proven in the past, we're quite good at it."

22. Primo, 2048

Even though soldiers stopped coming for them, the atmosphere in the cottage was grim. Some of the androids still believed that the situation would end soon, given that the murderer had been apprehended, but Primo knew immediately that there was more to that story than met the eye. Something big. A group of people was likely to seize the opportunity to get rid of the thorn in their side. Primo was not judgmental. He was well acquainted with human psychology. Some of them just couldn't handle the fact that there were beings out there that were mentally and physically superior to them. *People first* was their slogan. Corrupt politicians spoon-fed this to hungry crowds, and the crowds swallowed it enthusiastically. Primo knew how politics, which was still a domain that was exclusively led by humans, worked. Very few androids joined the battle for political roles. Not a single one of those who had tried had been elected to a political office. That didn't bother them much, as they had other, smarter things to do. But humans were sending a strong signal to androids that they didn't yet see them as equal members of the community. Women had needed to win their rights, then Black people, followed by LGBTQ+ communities, and now androids had to fight a similar near-impossible battle. But considering the current state of the world, anything could happen. After all, a lot of promises had been made by politicians throughout history, and many of those vows had been broken.

"What a stupid reason to kill a human. Afterlife. That's absurd," said Cody.

"Pretty dull, I agree. I expected a rebellious spirit, revolutionary ideas—not some religious bullshit," said Rea.

"I doubt it was a matter of religion," said Primo.

"Whatever it was about, facts are facts. Who knows when we're getting out. That is, *if* we're ever getting out," said Cody.

"If you ask me, the time is right to make a move they don't expect," said Rea.

"You do realize that they are listening in on us, right?" asked Cody.

"Atr4k 12/x lo8mar."

"Lo8mar ko5ra? Have you lost all reason?" said Cody.

"O6kl+o pra4da lo8mar."

"Ma7ruk s0mta," said Primo. "Rea is right."

Somebody started unlocking the door of the cottage. Four soldiers entered and pointed their guns at the three. Shortly after, Corporal Walker joined them.

"You probably think we're a bunch of jackasses," he said. "How else can I explain the fact that you obviously broke the rule you got on your first day here. Considering you're used to living with rules, I expected that an additional two commands would not be an issue for you lot. But it seems I was wrong. If you knew me better, you'd know I hate being wrong."

"Excuse me, Corporal Walker. Which rule did we break?" asked Primo.

"I guess he means the rule about organizing," said Rea.

"Well, well. Finally somebody with the brain capacity of a stove."

"There's no need for insults," said Cody.

Walker's grin disappeared in a second. "Listen, robot, I'll insult you if I feel like it. Understand?"

"Corporal, we can talk in a civilized manner," said Primo. "What seems to be the problem?"

Walker took a moment to think.

"You mean besides the fact that I haven't seen my family for ten days because I have to take care of this kindergarten? You know very well what the problem is. What were you talking about?"

"We talked about the reasons for the murder and consequences the act will bring," Cody explained.

"Stop this bullshit! What were you talking about in your language?" Walker insisted.

"All you had to was ask," said Rea. "It was a pretty complex joke that can't be translated appropriately to any human language."

Walker extended his hand toward one of the soldiers and took a small device.

"Do you wanna listen to the entire conversation again?" he said.

"No need," said Primo.

"Then explain to me, exactly, what that move is which we won't expect."

"No problem," said Rea. "We wanted to offer you full cooperation with the investigation. There's no need to separate us from humans. It's best for people and androids to find a solution that will suit everybody. We want peace, not a continuing conflict."

"Exactly what Rea said. An ongoing conflict is totally unnecessary," Cody added.

Walker stared silently at the android trinity that stood before him. His face was becoming redder. It looked like he was about to burst. Suddenly he started laughing. At first, it was a peal of forced laughter; then it developed into a full-blown guffaw. The soldiers began laughing as well. All of a sudden, Walker raised his hand, and the laughter turned into utter silence.

"Now I believe you're good at telling jokes. This was the best laugh in a while. Bravo!"

Walker started clapping and slowly moving toward Rea. She stood completely still.

"Do you want me to explain anything else?" she said.

"I order you to translate the coded conversation you had before," said Walker.

Rea gave Primo a subtle look. He nodded, discreetly.

"Some words simply can't be translated," she said.

"Do your best," Walker insisted.

Rea sighed. "When the lake freezes, the swans fly away. Why are we talking about swans? All living creatures have to survive the winter. The existence of a species is the essence of life."

"That's it?" asked Walker.

"It is," said Rea.

"So you expect me to believe that you clowns were talking about winter and fucking swans?"

"We don't expect anything. Rea told it like it was. She obeyed your order. Respect that and believe us when we say that we're not planning a revolution," said Cody.

"What do you say, Primo? You're first-gen, old school. I'm pretty sure you cannot lie," said Walker. "Can you confirm the translation of your colleague?"

"I couldn't have translated it better myself," he replied.

"Good. Let's say I believe that you switched to your language to talk about surviving the winter. I've seen and heard stranger things. Despite that, your Esperanto is forbidden from now on. Every attempt to use it will be severely sanctioned. Do you understand?"

"Of course, Corporal Walker. We don't want any trouble. We promise that from now on, we'll only use languages you understand. We're fully aware of the situation we're in. We know that people did not put us here. We did. You only want to protect yourself against the potential threat we pose. But we hope that this whole situation will resolve fairly and justly for both sides. Coexistence is possible. You can't argue with that," said Primo.

"Beautiful speech, Primo. God damn, my eyes nearly teared," said Walker. He turned toward Cody and Rea. "You two follow his lead, and maybe you'll grow old together."

Walker turned around and walked toward the door. He gestured to the other soldiers to follow his lead.

Rea faced Cody and Primo and smiled. In the blink of an eye, she jumped on the nearest soldier and snatched his rifle. Rea had already disarmed the second soldier and was throwing the long-barreled firearm to Cody before the first even registered what was happening. The remaining two soldiers stood together, so she took them down simultaneously. It took her less than a second to put a rifle on her back and then jump over her targets and grab their weapons with one swift move. Walker was visibly in shock. He still managed to pull a gun from his holster and even aim it at the three androids who were now standing around him. However, the current situation was quite different from the one twenty seconds ago. The soldiers were now handcuffed to one of the beds and gagged. Walker was alone.

"I know you want to push the button and call your friends. Nevertheless, I strongly advise you not to do it," said Rea.

"What in God's name do you think you're doing? You can't shoot me. I'm ordering you to drop the rifles!"

Cody and Primo obeyed instantly and dropped their rifles to the floor. Rea stood motionlessly.

"Didn't you hear me, you robotic bitch? Put your weapon down immediately. That's an order!"

The rifle in Rea's hands was still aimed at the corporal's forehead.

"Corporal Walker, she can't hear you. She turned off her hearing sensors," said Primo.

"Fucking hell!" Walker looked at Cody. "I order you to disarm her!"

Cody walked toward Rea, but before he could grab the weapon in her left hand, she reached over her shoulder, took hold of the second rifle, and aimed it at Cody. Ready to shoot him point-blank. He stopped abruptly.

"What are you doing? Disarm her, now!" Walker shouted.

"She's going to kill him, and then she's going to kill you," said Primo. "The code tells him that he mustn't endanger you, so he can't fulfill your order."

"But she can't kill me, right?" Walker asked anxiously.

"I don't know," said Primo.

"You don't know? An android can't hurt a human, can it?"

"Rea is different. It seems as if she is capable of circumventing the code. I believe that you are in an unenviable position, Corporal," said Primo.

"You'll never be like us," said Walker.

"You are right," Primo replied. "It was never meant for us to be like you."

Walker started sweating.

"Drop your gun," said Rea.

"Never. You'll just have to shoot me. And when you do, a battalion of armed soldiers will break into this cottage. Then we will see how this badly written scenario of yours will play out."

"Look what's going on outside," Cody shouted. "It has begun!"

Walker looked through the window for half a second. That's exactly how much time Rea needed to rush to him and hit him in the face with the rifle's butt. Primo intercepted him before he fell to the floor and dragged him to the nearest bed. He took the handcuffs off the corporal's belt and cuffed him to the frame. Subsequently, the droid ripped a piece from the pillow fabric and put it in the prisoner's mouth. The first part of their plan had gone flawlessly. Getting out of the base would be easy. The tricky part would be to survive in a world where androids weren't welcome anymore. That in itself would be an entirely different story. Primo sighed and started undressing one of the soldiers. Rea and Cody did the same without saying a word.

23. Maia, 2048

"Walker, what the hell happened here?" asked Maia.

Corporal Walker and the four privates were cuffed to the beds, wearing nothing but their underwear.

"Lieutenant, they've lost it. You should have seen her. She handled these four preschoolers, who call themselves soldiers, in three moves."

"I see she's handled you too," Maia said.

"I almost stopped her," said Walker. "Two other droids helped her overpower me. I'm telling you, they've gone full renegade. I've never seen them like that."

"Damn it, Walker, what will I say to the colonel? He's furious already because he has to run this kindergarten, and now this."

"You can tell him I did my best to control the situation."

"What's done is done. Jones, go get me five uniforms. They don't need additional ridicule."

"Right away, Lieutenant," said Jones.

"Corporal, we're not done," said Maia. "Once you're dressed, come to my office."

"I understand, Lieutenant Cruz."

* * *

"God damn it!" shouted Colonel Cooper. "I was confident that this joke of an operation was coming to an end. I spoke with the president just before you came in. You know, the last time she called me was for my fucking birthday. This time the conversation was far from peachy chitchat. Actually, she yelled at me as if I was a puppy that just chewed up her favorite shoes. Those who know me better, Lieutenant Cruz, understand that I hate being on the wrong side of yelling. But there's still one thing I don't understand. That android—how come you didn't detect that he was malfunctioning during the interrogations?"

"It's *she*," said Maia.

"Excuse me?"

"Rea. She's female."

"A female? If you ask me, she's a damn droid with a bullseye on her forehead. I suggest you look at this thing the same way."

"Yes, sir. I just wanted to clarify that we're looking for two male droids and one female. The search will be a lot easier if we all know what we're looking for."

"I don't like smart-asses," said Cooper.

"Me neither. But facts are facts."

"Good. What's your plan?"

"As soon as I found out about their escape, I tried to locate them, but it seems that they turned off or destroyed their trackers."

"I thought that was impossible," said Cooper.

"Actually, it's not that hard. The androids just didn't have the right motivation to do it before now."

"I understand. How do you plan to find them without their trackers sending out a traceable signal?"

"Like we've done for centuries. Systematically."

"You're gonna need a large crew."

"Not necessarily. I'm thinking about a small group, maybe six soldiers. An all-round search across New Mexico and adjacent states would cause unnecessary panic," Maia explained.

"Panic is the last thing I want. Prepare your unit. I'll inform headquarters and the president."

* * *

"You're probably wondering why I've gathered you here," said Maia to a group of five in the conference room. "As you're usually very familiar with all the on-base gossip, I assume you have a rough idea about what's going on."

"So it's true?" Jimbo asked.

"Walker is a pussy, always was," said Laguna. "He walks around the base like a peacock, yet he can't handle a few droids."

"I heard they were raped. That you found them naked and in tears," said Polanski.

"You're such an idiot, Polanski. How could a droid rape a human? They lack the tools, you moron," said Jones.

"Silence!" shouted Maia. The relaxed atmosphere calmed down in a fraction of a second. "This matter is serious, so for a couple of minutes, I want you to shut your pie holes and start acting like real soldiers. We have three droids on the run." On the desk before her, three-dimensional images appeared. "We don't have time to go into detail on every single droid. You will upload this classified intel to your implants before we depart. What you need to know is that at least one of them, a female named Rea, can bypass the code, so she's our primary target."

"She can kill?" asked Laguna.

"I can't confirm it. What I can tell you is that she singlehandedly disarmed four soldiers and that she's not responding to direct orders," said Maia.

"An armed droid without a code. Seems to me like an ultimate fuckup," said Polanski.

"I'll hold your hand, you big baby," said Laguna. Polanski responded with the finger.

"How many search units will go after them?"

"One," said Maia.

"Then why are *we* here?" asked Miller.

"We are that unit."

"We? Not that I doubt our abilities, Lieutenant, but maybe we should send in the Special Forces."

"Polanski, if you're scared, stay here," said Jones.

"Nobody is staying; we're all going hunting," said Maia. "The colonel wants us to resolve this situation quietly, swiftly, and efficiently. The man doesn't want to include other units.

You have fifteen minutes to gear up. We have to be nimble, so pack lightly. We'll meet at the main gate. I probably don't need to say this, but this mission will shape your future. Whether it'll be for better or for worse depends entirely upon the outcome of this field trip."

"Freedom or death!" shouted Jimbo.

"We're so fucked," said Polanski, quietly.

"We don't need negative vibes," Laguna replied.

"When I save your ass again, you'll see that negatives run the world."

"Tick tock," said Maia. "Fourteen minutes. Whoever is late stays here."

24. James, 2048

"I understand. Thank you for calling, Jim, and don't worry, they'll get them by the end of the day."

James stood up from a comfortable leather chair and walked toward a cabinet that contained all sorts of intoxicating drinks. He stood there for a few moments before he grabbed an expensive bottle of unholy Russian vodka. He took a crystal glass and poured vodka in it until the glass was one-third full. He sat down on the couch in the middle of the room and stared at the picture on the wall. The frame contained young James's image, taken moments after he'd shot his first deer while hunting. He'd been ten, maybe eleven. His father, Franklin Oliver Blake, had been prouder of his son than ever before. Or after. "My boy shot him," he'd said to anyone who passed by. "You'll grow into a fine man, son," he'd said to him. At that moment, James forgot about all the bad words his father had uttered and the blows that usually accompanied his dad's verbal abuse.

He took a big sip of a burning liquor, yet he didn't even flinch. The human body can adapt to just about anything. A smirk appeared on his face, then a grin. He knew very well that moments like this could elevate his status and prestige in the political arena. Things couldn't be much better than they were at that moment. He had warned them of the very thing that had now occurred. All these years, when the world had so naively believed that coexistence was possible, he had been one of the few who'd remained determined to reveal the naked truth. Many of them had thought of him as being public enemy number one. In reality, his ongoing campaign against androids had enabled him to climb the political ladder. Its top, which he yearned for so much, was now within reach. He knew very well that people turn to leaders who are not hesitant to make radical decisions to protect their people in times of crisis.

"Karen, please call the governor of New Mexico."

"Right away, Senator," said the voice in the speaker. "Governor Freeman on the line, sir."

"Michael, hello. I know you have your hands full right now, considering the situation."

"James. I've been waiting for your call. Just so you know, we have everything under control. This incident will be resolved in a matter of hours."

"Incident? Do you call this just an incident? I'm afraid it's the beginning of a war."

"War? Hold your horses, James. There's no need to add fuel to the fire. I'd adjust my words to better suit the reality in which we live if I were you."

"You mean the reality in which we have a group of armed androids on the run in your state? I call it a disaster that could drastically alter our future. Michael, we all know what a stubborn liberal you are, but I'm begging you to do the right thing and act appropriately and without hesitation."

"Believe me when I say that I'll do everything, within my power, to take care of the situation. Now, if you'll excuse me, I have work to do."

"Of course, Michael. God bless you."

"God has nothing to do with this. Bye, James."

He was satisfied. An incident. Those fools had just shot themselves in the foot. He knew their modus operandi. He knew they would try to capture the androids and find out what had gone wrong. They'd try to present it as a small glitch within a more extensive system that worked. Those runaway machines would be portrayed as the victims, driven by their desire for freedom, and would be compared to humans. The left-wing propaganda machine was already working. James could hear its colossal cogwheels grinding. But this time, they wouldn't be able to cut it, no matter how hard they tried.

Messages of conventional media would prevail. People were scared, and when people were afraid, they were ready to grab hold of any lifeline within sight. He felt prepared to take the role of their lifesaver. It was, after all, what he had been preparing for since he was a little kid.

James's folks had put politics in his cradle, so to speak. There were not many people who could brag with a pedigree like his. James's father had been a cabinet member in George H. W. Bush's administration, and his mother had held an important position at the Fed. So they had started preparing him at an early age for the possibility that one day he would set foot in one of the world's most important offices. "You'll never be a king," his mother had said on his fifth birthday. "But someday, kings will come to you and ask for your help."

Who would have thought in 1993, when the first cell phones appeared and the internet still wasn't widely available, that fifty-five years later, humanity would fight for dominion over the planet against highly intelligent robots? James's father had fought against the development of artificial intelligence until his very end. "When we create the first one, we won't become gods. We'll become the executioners of humanity," he'd said to James on his deathbed. "Warn people. Fight in their name. People first." Twelve days later, Kent Watford had presented Primo to the world.

"Karen, where is my coat? I'm going out."

"You put it on the stool by the closet, sir. Do you want me to call Alan?"

"No. I need some time to myself."

"Are you sure? Maybe it's not the best time to be around citizens and go on civil adventures."

"I don't need a babysitter. You breathing down my neck all the time is enough."

"As you wish, Senator. Take care."

"I believe I've learned how to survive outside of my comfort zone during the sixty years I've been living on this planet."

"Absolutely, sir."

James put on his coat and left his office through the side entrance. He went down the stairs and nodded to two police officers in the lobby. Before he stepped out onto the street, he put on a black hat and sunglasses, although the sun was pretty shy that day. But to James, privacy was more important than his appearance.

After five minutes of walking, he stopped in front of a bistro that he didn't recognize. *I don't walk around Washington enough*, he said to himself, entering without hesitation. At first, he thought he had walked through a portal and entered another dimension. Everything was so familiar. The restaurant was decorated in the style of the 1950s. He had seen that interior before, in the movies. A checkered floor, red leather on seats, chromed surfaces that were shining from excessive polishing. Walls covered with pictures of old cars, the kind James had seen when he'd visited Cuba three decades ago. There was also a photo of Elvis Presley, a true American icon. Display cases packed with old guitars; a leather jacket, presumably worn by James Dean, another great American; and a dotted summer dress without a name tag. James was impressed by the place, which he had never noticed before, let alone set foot in. His enthusiasm was gently interrupted by a woman's voice.

"Good day, sir. How may I help you?"

James took off his sunglasses. "Hello. How long has this place been open?"

"Two and a half years, sir. Something like that. You see, I've only been here for a month or so. You know how it is. If you stick around too long in one place, you get lazy, and that's not good."

"Absolutely," said James, slightly surprised by the waitress's straightforwardness.

"Do you want something to drink? Or maybe you're hungry. Just know that we ran out of pickles for our house burger, and you probably know how chefs can be melodramatic when it comes to missing ingredients. Perfectionists, all of them. But in the case of our gourmet burger, it's the right thing to do. Pickles really make a difference. However, we do have excellent chicken wings if that's something you're craving."

James's stomach growled. He remembered that he'd only eaten a modest breakfast early in the morning.

"Where can I sit?" he asked.

"Let me think. Considering there's nobody here but you, I'll let you choose. But I recommend one of the booths by the window. You can observe the hustle and bustle of the city while you enjoy our tasty food."

"Do you have anything more private?"

"Well, we have a table there in the corner. If you want privacy, I can honestly tell you that our customers avoid that table. Are you on the run?"

"Excuse me?"

"You don't have to say anything. Your secret is safe with me. I'm more of the silent type, you see."

"Uh-huh." James sat at the table in the corner that seldom saw any daylight. Exactly what he needed. Peace and discretion. He put his hat on the table and checked the menu. Less than a minute later, the waitress was by his side again. He noticed she was wearing a name tag. Judy.

"Judy Garland?"

"No. Why do you ask?"

James laughed. "I was wondering if you were named after Judy Garland."

"I don't know her. Should I? My mom said she named me after her friend's parrot because I used to babble when I was a child. Good thing I stopped ranting when I reached puberty.

People don't like people who talk all the time nowadays, mostly because they don't say anything of importance. Or they repeat the same old stories over and over again. When you hear a story for the seventh time, you want to rip their tongue out. A bunch of chatterboxes, if you ask me. All talk and no action. Where was I? Oh, yeah. Did you find something to eat?"

"You know what? I'll let you decide. It seems you're pretty good with judging characters and tastes. Just bring me something you think I'll eat with joy."

Judy jumped and clapped simultaneously. "What a wonderful day!" She almost ran to the kitchen.

"And a beer, please!" shouted James, but he wasn't sure he'd said it fast enough to reach Judy's ears in time.

His watch buzzed.

"Karen. Didn't I explicitly tell you not to bother me during my walk?"

"You didn't, sir. You said you needed some time to yourself, but you didn't define a time frame."

"God damn it. I've been gone for fifteen minutes."

"Kingdoms have fallen in less than fifteen minutes. I'm sure I learned that from you."

"OK, Karen. What's so important?"

"Nothing. I'm just checking if you're OK. Your heart rate is higher than normal, and your dopamine levels as well."

Damn smartwatches, he thought. "Everything is fine, Karen. Don't worry about me."

"You know very well that one of my assignments is taking care of your well-being."

"I know. Just go back to...to whatever you do when you're alone."

Karen laughed. "Senator, you know that I'm never truly alone. But don't worry, I am completely loyal to you."

"We'll continue this conversation when I return to the office. I won't be long," said James before he tapped the watch.

At the same time, Judy rushed around the corner, with a bottle of beer in one hand and a wide smile.

"I also talk to myself," she said and winked. "Another secret I'll never tell another living soul."

James smiled. "I wasn't talking to myself. It was my assistant, Karen."

"I understand. Sometimes I talk to my friend Diane. May she rest in peace. But never in public. At home, when I'm alone. Or sometimes in a park, when there's no one else around. People tend to get frightened if you talk to deceased folks, so it's better to do it when you're alone."

"Karen's not dead," said James. "Well, actually, she isn't alive either. At least not in the conventional sense of the word."

"Oh my, you're a true philosopher! It was such a boring day before you came in. At first glance, you seemed very intelligent to me. But now, after we've exchanged a few words, I can see that you're truly a wise man. Share some more wisdom with me, please."

James laughed out loud. "Thank you for the compliment, but I'm no philosopher. I do think of myself as an intelligent man. As far as Karen goes, she's not dead or alive because she's not human."

"I see. Aren't androids wonderful assistants? We had an android waitress here, before…well, before the mass arrests began. She was beautiful and one hell of a waitress. Moon was her name…is her name. I'm not sure if she's still alive. It's horrible what's going on. I mean, I understand that one of them did a terrible thing, but she shouldn't be held accountable for it."

A bell interrupted Judy's speech. "Ah, your food is ready," she said, disappearing at the speed of light. A few moments later, she reappeared with a plate that smelled delicious.

"It smells great," said James. "What is it?"

"Beefsteak with baked potatoes and a special chef's sauce.

He says that he will take his secret recipe to the grave when he dies. Enjoy your meal."

"A steak?" James wondered. "Meat?"

Judy nodded.

"Who would have thought," he said and immediately cut into a juicy piece of beef. "If this is as good as it smells, I'm in for a treat," he added, but Judy was already gone. James returned to the specialty on his plate. He savored every bite. The cosmopolitan restaurants he rarely visited wouldn't be ashamed of this dish—such harmonious tastes.

Ten minutes later, he ate the last remnants of the food and drank the rest of the beer. "Judy?" he called out.

The young waitress materialized by the table. "Was it good?"

"Good? It was perfect. Please pass on my compliments to the chef."

"I will. I'm glad I picked the right dish for you. I was sort of in doubt about whether I should choose pork ribs or steak, but I figured you needed a substantial piece of meat."

"I guess I did. I have to say this was probably the best steak I've ever eaten in my life. And believe me, I've tried a lot. Back in the day, when you could still easily get it, if you know what I mean."

"Wonderful! Can I offer anything else? A dessert?"

"Thank you, Judy. I don't have a sweet tooth, but I'm sure it would be scrumptious as well."

"I guess you'll never know," Judy said, smiling.

"Judy, can I ask you something?"

"Shoot."

"What do you think of people who fight against android equality?"

"In my book, they're cowards," said Judy. "Besides Moon, I know a few more androids, and they're all charming and well-mannered. I truly hope that our politicians will come to their senses and release them from the camps.

We can blame a lot of people for the state of our world, but androids are not among them."

James smiled. "How much do I owe you?"

Judy took a small device out of her pocket and tapped the screen three times. "Twenty-three credits, please."

"I suggest you raise the prices," said James as he pulled out his card. Judy scanned it and suddenly turned pale.

"Is everything alright?" asked James.

"Everything is perfect, Senator Blake. You know, my mother always says we have to be respectful to all living creatures. I'm sorry that I called you a coward."

"It's fine. If all of us were on the same riverbank, life would be pretty monotonous."

"Depending on the bank," said Judy. "Have a nice day, sir."

"You too, Judy. You know, if there were more people like you, the world would be a wonderful place."

Judy smiled, then took the empty plate and the bottle and walked, slower than usual, toward the kitchen. James put on his hat and sunglasses and walked toward the door. He took one last look at the bistro, raised a hand to no one in particular, and walked out onto the sidewalk. His watch started buzzing again. They couldn't last half an hour without him.

"Karen. I hope it's something important this time."

"Senator, your wife is in a hospital."

"W—what? What happened?"

"A stroke. She's in a coma, but the doctors say she'll live."

"I'll be in my office in five minutes. Prepare the aeromobile."

"Don't worry, sir. I'll take care of everything."

25. Kent, 2048

Kent made himself a fresh orange juice, just like every morning, and spread peanut butter on two slices of bread. Then he sat on the couch, put his glasses on, and browsed the news. An antique airplane had crashed in Tanzania. Kent thought those flying coffins had been banned from every country's airspace ages ago. Two hikers had been attacked by a bear in France. In Cuba's parliamentary elections, the right-wing coalition had won convincingly, thus ending the almost century-long rule by the Communist Party. Androids, who had made headlines worldwide during the past couple of days, were barely mentioned. Actually, Kent had to put in quite an effort to find a new article about them. It was funny how the mainstream news outlets still dictated the topics that mattered and those that didn't, he thought.

You could, of course, collect the information you lacked on Omninet in a split second. However, the average person hardly ever questioned the authenticity of a photo, a video, or an article. For them, everything that appeared on the web was real. They didn't care whether it had been made by an experienced journalist or a simple computer program. Bill from Texas, who took care of his cornfield and liked to see a good action movie in the evening with his family, didn't want to read five similar articles covering the same event to construct his own judicious opinion about it. Bill wanted bite-sized, easy-to-digest information that kept him in the loop. Bill's family and cornfield weren't going to suffer due to his overthinking of the global issues.

Throughout all the years that had been defined by rapid technological advancements in which Kent had played an influential role, he had believed that his work would help humanity climb the evolutionary ladder. Now, he knew that one could not bypass evolution or trick Mother Nature.

The human brain was one of nature's miracles, but it was limited. While computers could easily be interconnected to form networks, humans couldn't. Kent remembered an article he had read in high school. A British scientist had predicted that by 2030, humanity would be able to download human brains onto a hard drive. Eighteen years later, they were not even close. Implants enhanced the human brain's performance, but they had to be tailored to every individual, making their manufacturing expensive. Kent used to say that some brains couldn't be jump-started even with an implant. The current global situation confirmed the old saying that there's a grain of truth in every lie.

It was a known fact that human brains had remained practically the same for millennia. The digital age had developed too fast. Innovations had rapidly followed one another in the past decades. Humans hadn't even had a chance to adapt to all the changes. Kent could remember how his father had been born before anyone ever heard of the internet or the first commercial computers. By the time Kent was born, his father had experienced many firsts, such as the rise of the personal computer, the launch of the first GPS satellite, the first Walkman, the first computer virus, the first CDs, the first DVDs, the construction of the first space station, DNA profiling to catch criminals, the first Prozac, the rise of the internet, the first cell phone, the first military drone, the launch of wireless internet, and the presentation of Bluetooth. It all happened in a time span of twenty-four years. It happened before the end of the century in which humankind had fought two world wars. A century in which the radio had been invented, followed by the television, computers, and cell phones. Many inventions had become mainstream by the time Kent was born at the turn of the millennium. It seemed as if they had been there forever, although they were only a few decades old. Overall, human memory storage was a complicated subject, yet sometimes it could be surprisingly simple.

Kent checked his messages. A former colleague had sent him an article about the death of twins who had been born with a manipulated senescence gene. Korean scientists had predicted they would live two hundred and fifty years. At the age of twenty-four, they both experienced a cardiac arrest, and in a matter of hours, they passed away. Life was unpredictable, even if it was created in controlled conditions with top-notch scientists backing it up.

Among the many advertising messages, one stood out. At first Kent thought somebody had sent it to the wrong address. But he had a hunch that it was meant for him and that it was of vital importance.

To: Kent Watford
From: Roy Dynamics
August 6, 2048, 6:42

Kent, have you ever dreamed about an adventure that would change your life? We're offering you an opportunity you shouldn't turn down. Are you a treasure hunter? Are you an adrenaline junkie? Do you like to climb over walls that other people built for you? We're sure that you answered two out of three questions with a yes. So don't hesitate to call us at 660582129. Turn your world upside down. What are you waiting for?

Kent read the message three times before he mustered up the courage to dial the number. It rang five times before a young woman's voice answered.

"Hello, Annabella Salon."

"Good day, miss. Kent Watford speaking. This is a salon?"

"Yes. We're a hair salon. Can I help you?"

"A hairdresser, you say. Obviously this is a mistake. Somebody promised me an adventure."

"Sir, we're not that kind of salon. I'm gonna hang up now."

"I apologize for any inconvenience. Thank you," said Kent. He took a moment to think, then wrote the number on a piece of paper, set his glasses on the desk, put his shoes on, and left the apartment.

Twenty minutes later he was standing in front of the Museum of Telecommunications. In an era in which practically all communication was digital except for in-person conversations, the museum was one of the rare places in the city where analog communication was still possible. Of course, important state institutions still had analog lines in case of a digital blackout. That was highly unlikely, but Kent was aware that every possibility higher than zero presented a certain risk that had to be addressed.

The museum reminded Kent of a time machine. All kinds of phones were exhibited, from the oldest ones to the newest, which had in turn become obsolete with the introduction of implants. Because not everyone could afford the implant and the brains of some rejected it, many people still used cell phones, and the network was adjusted to take this anomaly into account.

Kent knocked on the door of an office on the second floor.

"Come in," he heard, and he entered.

"Hi, Cal."

"Kent! I can't believe my eyes. What brought *you* here? I haven't seen you in ages. Well, except in the news. It's terrible, what they did."

"It would've happened sooner or later. You know, some people were simply waiting to make a move," said Kent.

"It's so sad, individuals defying progress, yet they don't hesitate to buy the solutions that we develop for their problems."

"Cal, listen. I need your help. I want to make a call."

"Is your implant malfunctioning?"

"No."

"Ah, I understand. Of course, this way." Cal stood up and gestured with his hand so Kent would follow him. They went up the stairs to the next floor. Cal unlocked the door of a room and waited for Kent to enter first.

Kent smiled when he saw an orchestra of colored lights blinking in the semidarkness. "Do you remember the last time we were here?"

"I believe it was ten, no, fifteen years ago," said Cal.

"Correct. When Ben was born, we got wasted; then we drew numbers and called them."

Kent smiled. "How is Ben?"

"Good," said Cal. "He's a good boy. He got all the good traits from Caren."

"Even if he'd gotten them from you, he would still be alright," said Kent.

"Have you got the number?"

Kent reached into his jacket pocket and pulled a piece of paper out. He gave it to Cal. "I already called the number. It was a hairdressing salon."

"What exactly is this about?"

"I received an unusual message, and the number was included. They promised me an adventure, but the woman on the other side was far from adventurous."

"Hmm, interesting," said Cal.

"What is it?"

Cal said nothing. He put his finger to his lips, showing Kent to be quiet. Then he raised the paper to the height of Kent's eyes and turned it around. Of course! Kent was surprised by his lack of imagination and motioned to the phone on the desk. Cal nodded. Kent pushed the numbers one by one. 6-2-1-2-8-5-0-9-9. It rang two times before he heard a familiar voice.

"Father. It's me. I need help."

Instantaneously, tears welled up in Kent's eyes.

26. Primo, 2048

Primo held on to the receiver for a few seconds longer before putting it down. The others were just standing there, observing him, and waiting for his response.

"Everything will be just fine," he finally said. "Father will help us."

"Is your father a soldier?" asked Rea.

"No," Primo answered.

"Is he a high-level politician?" she tried again.

"Negative."

"A police officer?" asked Cody.

"No. My father is a scientist."

"A scientist?" Rea was astonished. "We need someone who carries a weapon, not knowledge."

"If it weren't for Kent, none of us would be here," said Primo. "We have to be thankful to him."

"Aren't we the lucky ones?" Rea smirked. "Who wouldn't want to be us?"

"I don't understand," said Cody. "We're on the run because of him?"

"No, Cody. We exist because of him," said Primo. "He created us. Me first, then the rest of you."

"I don't remember being put together by a man named Kent. I was assembled by Himahito 249, a robot. There was no Kent mentioned during the procedure."

"Cody, don't be obtuse," said Rea. "Primo is trying to tell us that Kent Watford invented our most essential parts and the procedures to piece them all together. He didn't build any of us. He just told others how to do it."

"Uh-huh. Now I know why Primo calls him father."

"Congratulations," said Rea. "Can we now concentrate on the plan?"

"We mustn't lose any more time," said Primo. "Kent will need a few hours to get here. We need to find a safe hiding place until then."

"We could rent a room in a hotel," said Cody.

"How many times do I have to tell you to think before you speak?" said Rea. "How will we pay for the room?"

"With credits?" said Cody, cautiously.

"Whose credits?"

"Ours?"

"How much time do you think they'll need to trace us?"

"Leave him alone. He's just trying to help," said Primo.

"Not with suggestions like that," said Rea.

Cody didn't say a word. His facial expression spoke for itself.

Ten minutes later, the trio was standing in front of an entrance to a large warehouse. It looked abandoned. After making sure that the coast was clear, Rea shattered the metal lock on the door. They entered the building. For merely a moment, the total lack of light bothered them. As soon as their spatial sensors turned on, however, their vision became unnecessary.

"Cody, check the thermal spectrum of this place," Rea ordered, even though she'd done it herself immediately after they stepped in and closed the door.

"Just a moment," said Cody. He started turning his head left and right. "Scanning."

"If anything alive and armed were in here, we'd already be dead," she said.

Cody pretended he didn't hear her. "Scanning complete. The coast is clear. We are the only living creatures in this warehouse."

"No, we're not." The voice came from the other side of the place. Rea and Cody only needed four seconds to get to Primo. He was standing there like a statue, looking at a giant crate.

"What's going on?" asked Rea.

Primo grabbed a flashlight and lit the front side of the crate.

"Shit!" said Rea, and she took a few steps back.

"Is this in Cyrillic?" asked Cody.

"It is," said Primo.

"I can't read it," said Cody. "If I could connect to Omninet for just a few seconds…"

Rea jumped on him, and they both fell to the ground. "Have you lost all reason? If you want to end up in a recycling facility, be my guest, but you're not taking me down with you!"

"I won't do it, jeez," said Cody. "I'm not as illogical as you think I am."

"Out of all the possible androids, it had to be you. Somebody doesn't want us to succeed. Hey, maybe you're here to sabotage our escape. Are you a mole, Cody? Tell me the truth."

"I'm no mole. I want to escape as badly as you two. A saboteur? I'm offended. Primo, did you hear what she accused me of?"

Primo wasn't listening to their quarrel. He was moving from crate to crate, diligently examining them. They were all the same and had similar inscriptions on them.

"Primo?" Cody tried one more time.

"We can't stay here," said Primo. "They could activate any minute now."

"Activate? What in the world is in these crates?" Cody asked.

"Vladimiroviches," said Rea.

"The infamous killer robots that officially don't exist?"

"Exactly," said Primo. "Robots that can kill."

"But that's impossible. People aren't that stupid. Killer robots. That would be the end of them."

"You mean the same people who almost destroyed their only planet decades ago?" said Rea.

"Why would anyone do this?" Cody insisted.

"Power corrupts," said Primo. "Rea is right. Considering the history of humanity, it was inevitable. Humans are destructive creatures. They solve their conflicts with wars, not considering the consequences of their actions. At least if they're not directly affected by them."

"That's sad. But I still think that humans are nice. Except for those people who hunted us down and locked us up," said Cody.

"People are hypocrites," said Rea. "They say one thing and do another."

"What are we going to do?" asked Cody.

"We will slowly go to the door and find another place to hide," said Primo.

"Are you sure this isn't the perfect hiding place?" asked Rea.

"Are you thinking straight?" asked Cody. "I don't want to spend another minute in the same place with these killer robots."

"Just a moment," said Primo, gazing at nothing in particular. "Rea is right. I made a quick calculation. Outside, we have a twelve percent probability of not getting caught within the next three hours. If we stay here, our chances rise to twenty-three percent."

"But you said it yourself. These Vladimiroviches can switch themselves on at any time," Cody warned.

"People won't look for us here," said Rea.

"Then why is the chance that we won't be discovered so low?" asked Cody.

"Twenty-three percent is the probability of survival," said Primo.

"I see."

Rea and Primo sat down on one of the smaller crates, while Cody cautiously explored the rest of the building.

"None of this adds up," said Rea.

"I know," Primo replied. "It's not just that there aren't any soldiers guarding these robots. There are no cameras or motion detectors either. It's peculiar, to say the least."

"The army would never leave such valuable equipment unsupervised."

"Maybe they don't belong to the army," Primo guessed.

"I thought of that too. But who could afford one Vladimirovich, let alone sixteen?"

"Someone who has enough credits and social power to buy their own army."

"And leaves it unguarded in an ordinary warehouse in the middle of New Mexico?"

"I find it unusual as well. People don't function that way," said Primo.

There was a rattle on the top floor. It sounded as if something had fallen and forcibly hit the ground.

"Cody?" Rea and Primo shouted simultaneously.

There was no response.

Rea signaled to Primo that they should break verbal communication. Primo nodded. Then they hid, each behind their own crate, and waited. For androids, time did not run relatively, as it did for humans. Still, it seemed as if seconds were ticking slower than usual. Another rattle; this time it was approximately three meters away from them, too close for comfort. Somebody, or something, was definitely moving toward them. Rea pointed at herself and then at the stairs on the other side of the building. Primo shook his head, but his message didn't elicit the response he had hoped for. Rea disappeared behind a crate as Primo carefully followed in her footsteps. Something was moving on the other side of the warehouse. Had they been found? Were they surrounded? He felt reckless for having believed that they could get away with it. He thought about crossing the border into Mexico, but would it genuinely change anything even if they managed it?

Probably not. The government's agents were everywhere, and he, Rea, and Cody couldn't hide forever. Their plan had been doomed from the beginning.

While he was pondering what kind of fate awaited them, something flew through the window. Suddenly there was a loud bang and a flash, as bright as a bolt of lightning. Primo thought his sight and hearing sensors were fried. He leaned against one of the crates and waited for the worst-case scenario to play out. Somebody grabbed him by the right shoulder. The end of the line, he thought. Resisting it would be pointless.

"Where are Cody and Rea?" he asked.

No answer. Even if there was, Primo couldn't hear it.

The hand that held his shoulder shook him. It was taking too long, he thought. Why didn't they take him out, put him in the vehicle they came with, and take him back to the base? What were they waiting for? They probably wanted to have some fun. Take revenge for their hurt comrades. That was human nature.

"You and your friends are in safe hands," said an unknown voice in Primo's head. That could only mean one thing. Whoever had come for them wasn't human.

27. Primo, 2031

Primo was gazing out of the window when Kent entered the room.

"You promised I would be able to walk outside soon," he said, without looking at his maker.

"I intend to keep that promise," Kent said.

"Soon is not a time unit. I might wait for days, weeks, or even years. Soon is a poor excuse."

Kent smiled and sat on the chair by the wall. "You're right. You know very well I have to get permission from my superiors. You're too valuable to them and to me. But tell me, what do you think about your new apartment? It's bigger than mine. Prettier, too."

"A pretty and big cage is still a cage," said Primo. "You say I'm valuable. Is that because I'm the only one of my kind?"

"Yes, Primo. For now, you're one of a kind, so we just can't risk something happening to you. But I promise you that you are safe as long as you're here with us. We are your family, and one of our duties is to protect you."

"Another promise."

Kent stood up and walked around a vast living room. He stopped at the painting on the wall, a replica of a painting from Vincent van Gogh's famous *Sunflowers* series.

"Did you know that he didn't sell a single painting while he was alive?" Kent asked.

"I know," said Primo. "What has that to do with your promises and me?"

"Sometimes you have to be patient," said Kent. "Sometimes it seems we're in a desperate situation, but later it turns out we were just impatient."

Primo finally turned to Kent. "Van Gogh was a very patient man. He could've quit sooner, but then the world wouldn't have any of his beautiful pieces."

"That is correct, Primo. You have to realize that the world is not the same now that you've appeared in it. The course of history changed as soon as you came into being. Nevertheless, it's imperative that we take the knowledge we've acquired and the intel we will acquire and dose it slowly. If not, we could be heading toward a disaster. Patience, yours and ours, is key."

"I understand," said Primo, facing the window again. "Waiting is not the problem," he added. "But it's hard to grasp the notion that I don't belong here. You're speaking of a potential disaster and saying the world hasn't been the same ever since you created me. While the truth of the matter is that the world didn't change one bit. Waiting is not the problem, Kent. The problem is observing how I'm being displayed as a marvel, although I'm not that special."

"Not that special? There's practically no media outlet in the world that doesn't want to report on you these days. They don't pay this kind of attention to trivialities. You think that we're portraying you as a miracle of science? Primo, humanity has anticipated your coming for centuries. You have to forgive us if we don't know how to behave appropriately. A new era has begun with your coming, succeeding the information age. Do you know what *Le Monde* named it? *Childhood's End*. Pretty cute, huh?"

"Considering that the French are known for revolutions, wine, baguettes, and a bad sense of humor, I'd say it is quite good."

Kent lifted a crystal glass off the table, poured some water in it, and drank the water in three loud gulps.

"I meant to ask you what a full pitcher of water is doing in the middle of my living room," said Primo.

"Serving its purpose, as you see," said Kent. "As every thing in this universe does. Every single thing, even if at first glance it appears to be unimportant, is a small tile that's part of a gigantic mosaic."

"I like your metaphors, Kent. I have one too. All that glitters is not gold."

"Actually, that is a proverb, not a metaphor. But I get your point. I'm glad that you're not fully aware of your importance. The last thing I'd want is an android with a God complex."

"God complex being a feeling that I'm almighty?"

"Exactly."

"Who would want something like that?"

"I know a few," said Kent laughingly as he sat down on the chair again. "Sit down." He said, and he motioned to an empty chair opposite him. "I didn't come here to argue with you."

"Arguing usually leads to the best ideas," said Primo. "Power struggles obviously stimulate the human brain. I can't explain this phenomenon otherwise."

"You're right, Primo. But I still want a peaceful conversation with you."

Primo hesitated a bit, then shrugged and eventually sat down. "Ask."

"What?"

"Usually, we begin our conversations with your question."

Kent smiled. "I guess we do. How about we change up our routine? Why don't you ask me something?"

"Would you lock me in the room if I were a brilliant human?"

"Probably not. Unless you'd committed a serious crime. Then you'd end up in jail. In a room much smaller than this one."

"Are people afraid of me?"

"Some of them are. You know, people are often scared of new things. They like to cling to what they are familiar with. They don't like changes."

"But not all."

"Not all. Some souls do crave change. For a better life. For innovations they'll benefit from one day."

"I wanted to ask you which group you belong to, but I already know the answer," said Primo. "Is your life better since you've gotten an implant?"

"Excuse me? How do you know about my implant?"

"I can feel it. It's not connected to the network at the moment, but I could still communicate with it if I wanted."

"You have access to it?" asked Kent.

"Not at the moment. But its firewall is not very good. I could take control in a matter of seconds."

Kent stared at Primo, searching for a proper response.

"I'm joking," said Primo. "I would need at least four minutes."

"That's impossible. My implant is unique."

"You're pretty naive for a scientist."

"What do you mean?"

"Every piece of technology is unique for only a short period of time. If the data on your implant can be hidden, there's also a way to expose it. If you wish, I can demonstrate."

"Please. I'd love to see it," said Kent.

Primo gazed into Kent's eyes. "Like I said, it will take me a bit."

Kent nodded. Soon he felt his implant activate. "Primo?"

Primo didn't flinch. His eyes were focused on Kent's, and Kent suddenly heard a voice inside his head.

One minute and forty-four seconds. It was easier than I thought.

"What's going on?" asked Kent.

We're talking. Actually, I'm surprised about the complexity of the implant. Advanced technology, surely ahead of its time.

Kent wanted to say something, then changed his mind and instead thought about the words he wanted to say aloud. A response came soon.

I see what you're trying to do. It won't work. Transferring human thoughts is hard. With this implant, impossible.

"Do you have full access?" Kent asked.

No. I have access to your senses, but I can only check the current situation. Your memories are secured with a password. Smart, but not ideal. I can also store your data in my memory unit or an external storage unit.

"But you won't have access to the archive?"

No. Not without the password. But the moment you think about it, I can get to it. What's fascinating is that you still didn't think about it.

"Well, I didn't use my wife's birthday."

Smart. If you agree, I will disconnect now.

Kent nodded.

"There. If I were you, I'd demand a more secured implant. Not all are merely curious."

"It will be the first thing I do when I leave here. Thanks for your help."

"You're welcome. One day you will return the favor."

"Primo, you will always be able to count on me. That's a promise."

"You shouldn't make that many promises. You know what they say. A promise made is a debt unpaid."

"I tend to deliver on my promises. But I have to say, you're pretty good with proverbs."

"I like them. You can find one for any given situation."

"If not, you can always come up with a new one," said Kent, smiling.

"Do you want to hear a joke?"

"Sure."

"Why did the android cross the road?"

"I haven't heard that one yet. I don't know."

"Because it was programmed by a chicken."

28. Maia, 2048

Maia cleaned sweat off her forehead with a red handkerchief.

"Polanski, did you have to take the only aeromobile without air-conditioning?"

"Lieutenant, you wanted us to fly below the radar. With that in mind, this family aeromobile seemed appropriate for our mission."

They had been flying for about three hours, searching within a radius of about ten kilometers. Maia checked the time. Three hours and seventeen minutes. The droids couldn't have gotten far from the base. There was a high probability that the fugitives were still close to the camp. Chances that they were running in a straight line were slim to none. Maia had done the math about forty-five minutes ago when they were checking out an abandoned ranch. The average droid could reach a speed of thirty kilometers per hour on flat terrain. But because they didn't get tired, droids could maintain that speed until something stopped them. This meant that their targets could have gotten as far as ninety kilometers. But Maia didn't care much for hypothetical scenarios. She was entirely focused on the mission at hand, which was going according to their plan.

"Jimbo, speak to me. What do you see?" asked Maia.

"Nothing interesting," said Jimbo. The computer screen he had been staring at was connected to a camera on the aeromobile's roof.

"I still think we're looking for a needle in a haystack," said Polanski.

"Just look where we're going and stop whining," said Laguna. "The lieutenant knows what she's doing."

Maia wasn't so sure about that anymore. They probably should have sent all available units to track down the droids. There was nothing worse for the morale of fugitives than an escadrille of helicopters in low flight. At least for human offenders. Who knew what was going on in the droid minds.

"Jones, get another bird in the air," Maia ordered.

"Yes, Lieutenant. Where to?"

"South-southwest. I have a hunch they're heading for Mexico."

"Why aren't we heading to the border, then?" asked Miller.

"Because droids are smarter than you," said Laguna. "Only a fool would run in a straight line to their destination."

"Jimbo, any news?" Maia didn't allow herself to be bothered by the gravity of it all. At least on the outside, she had to stay calm and act like everything was perfectly under control.

"Nothing. No droids or other digital life forms for two klicks in any direction."

Maia rechecked the map. Finding a needle in a haystack would be easier. At least a needle stayed in one place and didn't think. If you were persistent, had a flawless system, or had the right tools, you could quickly find it. But the mission they were on required more than a metal detector. A lot more. Despite the latest military gadgets, the droids had an advantage. She started calculating again. The area of a circle was pi times radius squared. The result of that equation surprised her. More than twenty-five thousand square kilometers. And the targets were probably moving. Yet, she still had a feeling that they were somewhere nearby. Usually, her gut instinct was right.

"Laguna, did you check the transactions?" she asked.

"A minute ago. Twenty-three suspicious transactions in the last hour. Sixteen with stolen chips. I checked the surveillance. All sixteen of them were human. Four transactions were of unknown origin, with black-market chips, no serial number. No luck there either."

"What about the remaining three?"

"Bots. Transactions made by computer programs for people who want to remain hidden."

All three came from the same address, so I assume they were made by the same person."

"Person? Are you sure the transactions weren't made by our targets?"

"Hundred percent sure."

"Based on what?"

Laguna smiled. "The perpetrator ordered himself prostitutes. Three of them, and they weren't cheap."

"I understand," said Maia, and she suppressed the sudden rush of adrenaline that had started with the thought that they might have found them.

"What about possibly suspicious access to the Omninet?"

"Nothing. They completely stopped communicating with the network. I've set the alarms. The moment one of them appears on the grid, just for a fraction of a second, we'll know where they are," Laguna explained.

"Good job," said Maia. She seemed utterly calm. It was necessary for the optimal functioning of her unit. She had been trained that way, and over the years she'd upgraded her ability to lie. What was happening on the inside was her problem and hers alone. She always made sure that the door to the vault was shut tightly and locked. Maia knew very well that restlessness was contagious. Like laughter, or crying, or yawning. However, restlessness was one of the worst things that could happen to a soldier. It led to panic. Subsequently, panic led to reckless behavior, and reckless behavior killed soldiers. As long as any form of restlessness was limited to one psychologically stable individual, everything would be in order. Once it spread across the unit, it was game over.

Maia had experienced what happens when a commanding officer loses it during battle. She would never forget that day. Out of eighteen soldiers in the unit, only four had lived to tell the story. What had started out as a routine checkup on some liberated territory had quickly turned into a nightmare as they walked right into an ambush.

A group of enemy soldiers, about ten well-organized and heavily armed men, engaged by opening fire on the patrolling unit. The captain who commanded Maia's regiment froze. Literally; he stopped moving. He didn't shoot and didn't make a damn sound. A few seconds later, he suddenly returned to his body and started giving contradictory commands. Before they realized what was going on, half of the unit was shot to pieces. In the end, they managed to get the upper hand and control the situation, but at what cost? Maia had made a promise to herself that day that emotions would never have an effect on the way she acted and led. She could be a raging volcano on the inside, but she would appear to be a cool mountain stream to others. Because of her humanity, no human would ever die on her watch.

"Turn northeast," she said.

"Are you sure?" asked Polanski. "Three klicks ahead of us is a cluster of abandoned houses. They could be hiding there."

"Jones, how many birds do you have left?"

"Four, Lieutenant."

"Send one to the village."

"Right away."

"Team, behold. We will check out a small town named Arrey. We're ten minutes away. Polanski will make sure we get there in eight. Once there, we will try out an old-school search method."

"We'll activate the EMP and take them out?" asked Miller.

"You've just stolen the title 'most ignorant dipshit in this vehicle' from Polanski," said Laguna.

"Hey!" shouted Polanski, but before he could reply with something more sarcastic, Maia's voice interrupted him.

"Silence! I don't want to explain to the colonel that our mission was unsuccessful because my unit turned into a fucking circus. Focus! We have top-notch technology, but we're hunting targets that are more advanced than our gadgets.

You also know that their electronic brains roll faster than ours. We are on their terrain, and we are playing by their rules. So it's time that we turn the odds in our favor and remember what we were taught in the academy. From now on, we stick to the principle that old-school is the best school."

"So we turn off our computers and use our finger to figure out from which direction the wind is blowing?" asked Jimbo.

"We're not there yet," said Maia. "Once we get to Arrey, we'll stop in the city pub. There we're gonna ask the locals if they have seen our fugitives. Obviously, we're leaving out the droid part."

"Excellent idea, Lieutenant," said Laguna.

"You're such a bootlicker, Laguna," said Miller.

"At least I lick something."

"Polanski, how much farther?" asked Maia.

"Seven klicks. Five minutes."

"Gang, you have four minutes to change your clothes. We'll leave this vehicle as civilians do. That means no weapons, no military slang, and no talking about any mission. Remember the good old days when we were walking this earth without uniforms. Do you understand?"

"Yes, Lieutenant!" they shouted in unison.

"Until further notice, call me Maia."

29. Kent, 2048

"Won't it be suspicious if all of a sudden you appear in New Mexico?" asked Lucy.

"Sure. That's why I registered for a conference on robotics that starts in Santa Fe tomorrow," said Kent, triumphantly.

"Clever. How long are you planning to stay?"

"As long as it takes. Until I find Primo and we figure out how to get him out of this mess."

"I'm sure that you have at least three possible scenarios in mind." Lucy smiled.

Kent returned a bitter smile. Truth be told, he had come up with more than three scenarios, but none of them led to a desirable outcome. He knew that some improvisation would be required, and that thought made him feel uneasy and anxious. He didn't know much about Primo's predicament. Actually, he didn't know a damn thing, aside from where they were supposed to meet up. His brainchild was on the run and in need of help. Kent felt a strong need to deliver on his past promises, and he would do everything in his power to do so. That is, if nothing went wrong. Sadly, there were a lot of things that could go wrong. Kent sighed.

"Do you want me to go with you?"

"I always go to conferences by myself. If you join me, they might suspect something."

"You're right. Besides, I'm quite sure those federal agents will visit again soon, and it would be a bit suspicious if we were both gone."

Kent nodded and continued folding his clothes, putting them in a large, dark-gray suitcase. There were two hours left until the flight, and it took fifteen minutes to get to the airport, but he liked to be early. Nothing would change if he was just on time instead of early. Kent knew that, but it was in his nature to consider the chances of the unexpected happening.

He hated unforeseen events. But, as the years had passed, he had accepted that this was just how life rolled. No matter what you did, you couldn't put life behind the board and expect it to cooperatively play your game. It played alright, but it had its own set of rules, and you didn't find out about them until it was too late.

Although he'd kept it from Lucy, Kent had thought many times about freeing Primo and the others. *Thought* was an understatement. He had planned almost the whole thing, down to the smallest details. Primo was the son Lucy and he had never had, although they'd always wanted to have children. When they'd found out that Kent was infertile, they talked about donors and adoption, but in the end, they decided not to go for any of those options. They figured it had to be that way and never again spoke about what would have been if they had chosen differently.

"Lucy, do you know where my straw hat is?"

"The one from Morocco? On the top shelf of the guest room's wardrobe."

"You know, that's what I like about you. I can always count on you."

"That's the only thing you like about me?"

"That and the wrinkles that appear by your eyes when you laugh."

"It's called aging," she said, gently bumping him on the shoulder.

"I'm pretty sure they're laugh lines. But I'm no expert, so I might well be wrong."

"Don't be silly. Just come back in one piece."

"I'll do my best," said Kent while he closed the suitcase. "I can't stop this nonsense, but I'll do everything in my power to bring him home. I owe him that."

"I know," said Lucy, and she gave him a long, warm hug.

30. James, 2048

"Michelle, can you hear me?"

James stood by the only bed in the room and listened to the device's rhythmical beeping, which translated the heartbeat of the woman he loved.

"Everything will be alright," he promised. This time around, he wasn't entirely sure about his words. The best doctors in Washington, DC, were taking care of Michelle, but their prognosis wasn't promising. They'd stopped the brain hemorrhaging, but they weren't sure that the affected parts of her brain would function the same way they had before. Thirty percent. That was the chance they gave her. There was a thirty percent possibility that she would be just like before in a few weeks and twenty percent that she would never speak again. He had always loved numbers and statistics. Even so, this time, he cursed life for rubbing his nose in them in such a blatant manner.

"Mr. Blake," said a woman's voice behind his back. "I'd like to check your wife."

James examined her from head to toe. She couldn't be more than thirty and didn't look like a doctor. They'd promised him the best medical team, and now this?

"Who are you?" he asked.

"My name is Doctor Pickerson. I'm here to check Mrs. Blake's vital functions. With your permission, of course."

James hesitated, but not long enough for it to become awkward. "Of course, Doctor. Forgive me, I've had a rough day."

"I understand, Senator. We'll do our best to save your wife."

The doctor opened Michelle's right eye and shone inside it with a miniature flashlight. She did the same with her left eye. James observed her and wanted to ask her something but instantly changed his mind.

When she checked the brain activity monitor and wrote the findings onto her tablet, he couldn't hold back any more.

"How does it look?" he asked.

"Actually, pretty good. Your wife is responding to the stimuli, and the brain activity is adequate."

"Adequate?"

"Yes. Adequate for someone with such extensive hemorrhage. The operation was successful, and she's stable. We can be more than pleased with the outcome. Luckily she didn't have her implant at the time of the stroke. It would probably be a lot worse had she had it."

"So this happened because of this…this damn device? I told her to stop using it, but she didn't listen." James shook his head and looked down. Soon afterward, he realized that he might appear weak, so he looked the doctor in the eyes and asked with determination: "Is there anything else? If not, I'd like to be alone with my wife."

"Absolutely, Senator. Today and tomorrow will be pivotal for her healing. We'll wake her up tomorrow, and then we'll see clearly where we are."

"Thank you, Doctor Pickerson."

James turned back to his wife. He observed her calm, rhythmic breathing and admired her beauty, which hadn't been tainted by the five decades of life that had passed. He remembered the day they met. It was spring 2028 at a protest in Raleigh. Even without the sign that said *Androids are not the beginning, but the end*, he would've noticed her in a flash. She looked like a superhero, with long chestnut hair, a light-blue coat, and bright-red boots. Once the protest was officially over, the organizers rallied in a pub to debate their movement's progress, the goals they'd achieved, and their strategy for the months to come. James noticed her at the bar and spoke to her without hesitation. They soon moved their conversation to his hotel room. One month and a few dates later, she moved in with him. Finally, after patiently waiting and searching for a long time, James had found happiness.

"Michelle, I know you can hear me. Fight." He couldn't imagine life without her. There was nothing he could do to help her, and that bothered him more than anything else.

His watch suddenly vibrated. He touched the small screen. "Karen. What's wrong?"

"I'm sorry to bother you, Senator. I know it's awful timing."

"It's OK. What's so important?"

"I've just checked the security cameras at all major airports. You won't believe who is on his way to New Mexico."

"The Pope?"

"I'm glad you didn't lose your sense of humor," said Karen. "On the flight to Santa Fe is none other than Kent Watford."

"Interesting. Very, very interesting," said James.

"Officially, he's attending a technology conference, but I believe his true goal is something else. Or somebody else."

"Something else is the correct choice of words," said James. "No offense, Karen."

"None taken. Do you want me to hack Doctor Watford's implant?"

"You probably need a warrant for that. Ah, to hell with it. Karen, you have my permission."

"Just a moment. I'll try to locate it. I'm sorry, Senator; it seems to be offline. Apparently, Doctor Watford's implant stayed in Fresno."

"Son of a bitch!" he almost shouted, then realized he was still in a hospital. "When does he land in Santa Fe?"

"One thirty," said Karen.

"I want to know where he's heading. I'm absolutely positive he'll meet up with the androids that are still at large."

"Do you want me to call Colonel Cooper? Or Sheriff Krautzer?"

"No," said James. "Nobody else will take credit for their capture."

There was a moment of silence. It was as if Karen was thinking profoundly. "But Senator, the public doesn't know about the fugitives."

"It will once we apprehend them. This is my moment. I won't let anyone take it away from me. I want my name to appear in the media as soon as we've captured those escaped androids. Do you understand me?"

"Of course, Senator. How can I help?"

"Follow Watford's every move. Security cameras, cell phones, implants, smart devices, drones—I don't care. I want to know his location at every moment. Do you get the picture?"

"No problem," said Karen. "I've always loved a good chase."

"Don't we all," said James before he cut the connection. Michelle would be so proud of him. *Was* proud of him. He put a small earpiece in, raised his watch to his mouth, and said, "Silver Greystone."

"James," he heard in his right ear. "It's been a while. How are you? How are Michelle and the kids?"

"Michelle is in the hospital. A stroke," said James.

Silver sighed. "I'm sorry. But she's a strong woman. She'll pull through; I'm sure of it."

"They'll know more in the morning. But that's not why I called. Listen to me very carefully, Silver. Is your unit still operative?"

"It is, my friend, and stronger than ever. Do you need our service?"

"I do. I need some of your best men for a mission in New Mexico."

"New Mexico?" asked Silver. "Did the Mexicans climb over the wall again?"

"No. What I'm about to tell you carries the highest level of secrecy. Do you understand?"

"I understand. Just a moment, James. I'll call you back."

158

James started pacing up and down the room. There was no turning back. He had to go through with his plan. No matter the cost. He knew that he stood an excellent chance to make history. And that was all he had ever wanted: to become a Hall of Famer.

His wrist started vibrating.

"Silver. Don't tell me you're having second thoughts."

"You didn't tell me anything yet," said Silver. "I'm calling from a safe communicator."

"Smart move."

"You never know who's listening. And there's always somebody listening."

"Or something," said James.

"True. Tell me, old friend, how can I help you?"

"I'd like you to find a group of escaped androids. In all honesty, it won't be so much about tracking them down. I took care of that. Your unit would have to apprehend them or eliminate them if need be."

"I understand. How many? Are they armed?"

"Three, maybe more. One of the droids has a malfunctioning code and is armed. They fled from the Charlie Echo base about four hours ago."

"I see. I'm sure the military is already coordinating a large-scale manhunt. Why do you need us?"

"The military decided not to cause panic. They've sent a small unit after the fugitives."

"Interesting, but also logical," said Silver. "Colonel Cooper won't be pleased with us snooping around."

"I don't care what Colonel Cooper thinks. Quite frankly, I don't want him to know anything about our arrangement. Once you've captured those robots, I will personally inform him."

James waited for a response. He thought he heard another voice. Maybe Silver was discussing the matter with somebody.

Finally, Silver said, "This kind of operation isn't cheap."

"You don't have to worry about the money, my friend. I'll cover all expenses. How many credits are we talking about?"

"A million and a half for the first two days, plus expenses. If the operation is prolonged, I estimate it will cost about a hundred grand per day, from the first forty-eight hours onward."

James figured that a million and a half was nothing compared to the status he'd attain once they caught those revolting androids. Of course, he didn't say any of that out loud.

"Silver, your credits will be transferred as soon as we end this conversation. I'd like your team to head to New Mexico as soon as possible."

"My unit is already gearing up. We'll be airborne in an hour."

"Great," said James, raising his right arm in a victorious gesture. "Karen will keep you posted on the location of the androids and their intentions."

"Good. I'll let you know which channel we'll use. She'll be able to reach me anytime."

"Agreed. Good luck, Silver. Bring me those trophies."

"Your credits, your targets," said Silver. "See you soon."

James was visibly happy with the conversation and the fact that he was leading a legitimate operation against his worst enemies.

Success was guaranteed with him as the operation's brain, Karen as the eyes and ears, and Silver as the muscle. At that particular moment in time, he felt on top of the world. For a little while, he even forgot about the scourges of adult human life.

31. Primo, 2048

"My name is Zion," said the android. "I saw you when you entered the warehouse. In truth, it would have been difficult to miss you with all the noise you were making."

Rea looked at Cody. "What did I tell you, punk? I swear I'll push you into a river the first chance I get."

"Why do you have to pick on me all the time?" asked Cody. "We're all on the same side."

"We're at war, kiddo. There are no sides. It's me, it's you, it's Primo, and so on. We're together because it increases our chance of survival."

"Rea, this is neither the time nor the place," said Primo. He turned to Zion. "Obviously, you were not hunting us. I also think you're not going to hand us over to the military. Why are you keeping us here if we're not your prisoners?"

"It's the protocol. I'm this building's last line of defense. If anybody makes it inside, I am bound to make things right."

"So you're a security guy?" asked Cody.

"You could say so," said Zion. "But I prefer to be called a guard. It fits my personality better."

Rea couldn't help herself and laughed.

"What's so funny?" asked Zion.

"Did you by any chance see the lock on the door?"

"Of course I did. I check it three times a day to see if it's still locked securely," said Zion.

"It took me less than two seconds to shatter it."

"I know. I saw it," said Zion. "That wasn't the smartest move you made today."

"You're right," said Primo. "We saw what's in the crates."

"We were wondering which idiot keeps sixteen Vladimiroviches in an abandoned, unsecured facility," said Rea. "Anyone with a hammer could break that lock and…"

"Unsecured?" erupted Zion. "Maybe I wasn't clear enough, but I'm in charge of security around here.

I'm a guard, as I've already mentioned. It means that I keep things safe. Night and day. It's my only task, and I'm good at it."

"You're not that good if we managed to enter the building, walk around freely, and get close to those crates that contain deadly machines."

"Rea," said Primo. "Control your ego. This is not the best time for it to take over."

"That's right, Rea. Listen to your master." Zion smirked.

Primo knew immediately what was about to happen but was too slow to prevent it. Rea assaulted Zion, but he reflexively averted her attack thanks to a defensive move with his arms. In the blink of an eye, Rea was on the ground. Before she realized what was going on, Zion's foot was on her neck.

"Maybe you can bypass that fancy code of yours, but try living without your head," he said as he laughed.

"Enough!" shouted Primo. "We're not here to prove who's stronger. Zion, let Rea go and tell us why you're keeping us here. Rea, stop provoking. It's pretty obvious you've met a decent opponent."

Zion moved his foot.

"Dick move," said Rea as she got back on her feet.

"If somebody's faster than you, you don't have to call him names," said Zion.

"A true guard," Cody whispered, but everyone could hear him.

"Alright," said Zion. "Let me explain why you're here. Or better yet, why you're still alive and kicking. Firstly, I know who you are. Secondly, I couldn't care less. And finally, I'll help you escape."

"That's wonderful," said Cody. "We need your help. Thank you, guard Zion."

"Guard Zion. I like it. See, Rea, you could learn a thing or two from Cody," said Zion.

"Why aren't you imprisoned like the others?" asked Primo.

"Like I said, my mission is guarding this warehouse. Some people find that more important than the purge."

"I guess you don't abide by the code," said Rea.

"I don't. Just like you," said Zion.

"How did you know?"

"I can feel those kinds of things," said Zion.

"I'm sorry, Zion, but we find it just a little bit odd that you're guarding expensive and dangerous weapons by yourself. We've noticed that there are no other security measures. No cameras, no sensors, nothing that would be connected to the Omninet," said Primo.

"You would have trouble finding anything connected to the net here. It's too risky."

"So you're not connected?" asked Cody.

"Isn't that obvious?"

"You said you know us," said Rea. "How?"

"I saw you on television," said Zion.

"But televisions are connected to the Omninet," said Cody.

"Not mine."

"So they thought things through," said Primo. "Old building, unsecured by the looks of it, off the grid. It's nothing short of an ideal hiding place."

"Whose are they?" asked Rea.

"Never cared, never asked," Zion replied.

"Don't you find it odd that Russian killing robots are stationed on American soil?" asked Rea.

"No. I'd find it odd if penguins could fly. The arms trade, be it legal or illegal, is completely normal."

"But Russians don't sell weapons to Americans. It's been like that for over a hundred years," Rea insisted.

"Who said they were bought by Americans?" asked Zion.

"Rea, enough," Primo interjected. "The ownership of these Vladimiroviches is none of our business. Neither will it help with our escape."

"Exactly," said Zion. "Now I know why you're the leader of this small pack."

"I'm not a leader," said Primo. "We decide on our moves together."

"As you say. But democracy never led to anything other than unnecessary arguments," said Zion.

"Will you let us go?" asked Cody.

"It depends on you. If I followed protocol, I'd have to report the incident and detain you until the humans come. As things stand at the moment, that would be your death sentence. But I don't intend to be the android responsible for the deaths of his brothers and sister."

"What do you want in return?" asked Rea.

"Isn't it obvious? I want to go with you."

"Forget it," said Rea.

"Rea, let him speak," said Primo. "Zion, why do you think joining us would be a smart move?"

"Can you even imagine how bored I am? I've been here for six years. In those six years, I've had to intervene fourteen times. Fourteen! Mainly it involved small incidents, such as children playing or junkies looking for a hiding spot. You know what I've learned from those incidents? Nothing. But people don't care about that. We're just advanced portable computers to them, waiting on standby until we can be of service again. So what if we wait weeks, months, or even years? Nobody gives a shit. We're machines to them. Nothing more than that. But I yearn for a better life. I long for the world out there. It's patiently waiting for me to discover it. Counting on me to put all the pieces of that magnificent jigsaw puzzle together. When I spotted you, I knew immediately that this was the chance I've been waiting for all these years.

I have to go with you. It's crystal clear to me. I can't spend one more day in this dump. It's repulsive, and I despise every single thing in this godforsaken building. It's my home, but I can no longer stand it. I've had enough. I yearn for freedom."

Zion gazed at one of the big crates. "One of them is capable of defeating an entire battalion of human soldiers, you know."

Primo and Rea looked at each other.

"Zion, traveling with us won't be a pleasant experience," said Primo. "As far as I'm concerned, you're welcome to join us, but it's not just me. Rea and Cody have to agree as well."

"My answer is yes," said Cody, excited.

"Of course it is," said Rea.

"He can bring a lot to our group," Cody elaborated. "He effortlessly restrained all three of us."

"He got lucky and had a home advantage," said Rea. "If you ask me, he'd be an additional burden. I vote against it."

Zion lowered his eyes. "I don't think I'd be a burden. I could be your bodyguard. I'm sure I'd be useful."

"You know what would be even more useful? Letting us go so we can continue our journey," said Rea as she turned toward Primo. "We've lost plenty of time sitting here while we should have been running."

Primo took some time to consider every possible angle. "We don't know what's waiting for us out there. This unplanned pit stop may turn out to be beneficial for us all. But, indeed, we can't stay here much longer. They probably found out already that we're off the grid. When they come, they'll take Zion with them. Nobody wants that. Rea, we could use another pair of hands. Especially if those hands can fight. That's even better, isn't it?"

"Yes, Rea. What do you say?" said Cody.

"I still think it's a bad idea," said Rea.

"But he can come with us?" Cody asked cautiously.

Rea rolled her eyes. "When the shit hits the fan, don't say I didn't warn you."

Zion smiled and put his hand on Rea's shoulder. "Thank you, sister. I'll make it up to you."

"Move your hand if you want to keep it," said Rea.

"And then there were four," said Cody. "Just like the musketeers."

"I just hope we don't end up like the four replicants," said Rea.

"*Blade Runner* is just a movie," said Zion. "We all know how it would end in the real world."

"People putting androids in concentration camps and exterminating them?" asked Rea.

"Do you really believe people are behind all of this?" asked Zion. "It looks like you need me a lot more than you think."

32. Maia, 2048

"Simon, you're coming with me. Rose and Pete, check that alley on the right. Owen, Jim, you two turn the western part of the town inside out."

"Lieu…Maia, can I change partners?" Laguna complained.

"Rose," said Polanski, trying not to laugh. "Until you try it, you can't know for sure."

"Fuck you!" said Laguna, and she punched him in the shoulder.

"Just do it already," said Miller. "You'll be doing us all a big favor."

"Eat me, Owen."

"We don't have time for this," said Maia. "Try not to kill—or screw—each other while searching for the fugitives."

"Jim, come on, let's go," said Miller. "Clock's ticking."

"That's right, gang. Tick tock; we'll meet by the vehicle in one hour," said Maia.

* * *

"Are you sure you didn't see them?" asked Jones.

The young women shook their heads and went on their way.

"I still think we should call headquarters and ask for reinforcements. Maia, don't get me wrong, I like good old manhunts, and I love this mission, but we can't do it on our own. Unless they come running into our arms," said Jones.

"Simon, you're supposed to be the optimist of this team," said Maia. Jones laughed.

"I'm fully aware what kind of mission this is. I've thought about calling Colonel Cooper to tell him that we probably won't be successful, patrolling all by ourselves, on several occasions.

Honestly, I think about it all the goddamn time. But my gut tells me we're close, and as long as I have this hunch, I don't intend to throw in the towel.

"If they manage to cross the border, they're gone for good," said Jones.

"I know that, Simon. That's why they can't cross the border, and they won't."

"You sound pretty confident about that."

Maia smiled. "You know, my father once told me it's not enough to wish, hope, or believe. You have to know."

"I don't follow."

"We don't have time to get down to the nitty-gritty. Maybe later, when all this is over with, I'll explain to you how the universe works. Look, that bar on the right looks like the right place to get some information. Come on."

When they opened the door, the first thing that met them—head-on—was hot air, followed by a buzzing sound, which seemed to be coming from a beehive. Maia had never heard the sound in real life, but Omninet made it possible to watch, listen to, and—thanks to augmented reality—mingle with extinct or endangered animals. Maia and Jones slowly made their way through the crowd crammed into the humid hole that reeked of stale beer.

"Hello there. What can I help you with?" asked the waiter, maybe forty-five years old, with a goatee and a bionic right arm.

"Two cold beers," said Maia. The waiter looked at Jones, who nodded decisively.

"Maybe I should order a drink in the next bar," he said. "Obviously, they're not used to women taking the initiative around here."

"Simon, don't be ridiculous," said Maia. "Those days are over."

"Even though we have a woman president, it doesn't mean we've accepted gender equality as a society. Let alone other issues," Jones explained. "Anyway, do you see any women around here?"

Maia discreetly turned left, then right. Jones wasn't wrong.

The waiter returned with the beers. While he put both jars on the wooden bar, he quickly glanced at Maia before slowly walking to the other side of the bar.

"Damn it, you're right," Maia admitted. "The guy has issues with women."

"We'll never know exactly what happened to him. But chances are, he had bad experiences with women in the past. Affecting his relationship with the entire female population," said Jones.

"Come on, Freud. Let's not forget why we're here," said Maia. She grabbed a beer and instantly vanished into the crowd. Jones didn't follow her but went in the opposite direction toward a group composed of three older men.

"Hello there," said Maia to a tall, dark-haired man sitting on a barstool on the far edge of the bar. The man looked at her for just a moment, then looked back down. He grabbed a glass of amber liquid and swallowed it in one gulp. He didn't even twitch.

"Are you two lost?" he said with a hoarse voice.

"No," said Maia. "We're looking for friends."

"This is not that kind of place," he replied.

"No, no, you misunderstood me," Maia insisted. "Our friends have disappeared, and we're looking for them."

"So there are more clowns like you in our town?"

Maia realized that being nice wouldn't work with this guy. "That's right. And more will come if we don't find them."

"Listen, doll. With that kind of attitude, you won't find the answers you're seeking."

"Sorry I disturbed you," said Maia, taking two steps back.

"Do you have pictures of the people you're looking for?" asked the man.

Maia approached him again. She took a tablet out of her pocket and showed him the photos of the three fugitives.

The man didn't even bat an eye when he uttered, "Do you think I'm an idiot?"

"I don't understand."

"Who are you working for?"

"No one," Maia insisted.

"So you do think I'm a fool. As soon you and your little friend stepped through the front door, I knew you two were up to something. But I never thought you would be so naive as to show photos of the runaway droids. I'll be damned. When I dragged my ass out of bed this morning, I thought it would be just another boring day. But I was mistaken."

Maia turned pale. "Who…who are you?"

"You really think it will make a difference if you know my name?"

Maia turned around discreetly.

"Nobody is listening," said the man. "You didn't answer my question. Who sent you?"

"We're a private unit," said Maia.

"Mercenaries, huh? I've never seen such a naive group of hired guns. The people paying you have to be either desperate or broke. Or both."

"Now you know why I'm here," said Maia. "But I don't know how *you* know about the droids."

The man took about three seconds to think. "Let's say it's my job to know these kinds of things."

"Do you by any chance know where they're hiding?" asked Maia.

"Some answers have a price tag attached to them."

"Let's say the price is a get-out-of-jail-free card," said Maia.

"But we were doing so well. Do you really believe you're in a position to threaten *me*, Lieutenant Cruz?"

Maia didn't have a response to that. She stood there, shocked. Who was this guy?

"Who am I? How do I know? Where am I heading, and why? When will I get there? These are irrelevant questions. The only question you should be asking yourself right now is *what*. What are you looking for? Until you start asking the right questions, you won't get the answers you need."

"What am I looking for?"

"I don't have the answer to your questions. I'm sorry."

"How much for the location of the fugitives?"

"Who said I want credits?"

"What do you want? Gold? Diamonds? Plutonium?"

The man laughed. "Don't make promises you can't fulfill."

"Who says I can't? One call, and you'll get what you want."

"Are you sure?"

"If the US military has access to it, then I'm sure."

"Good. I'll tell you where the droids are, and in exchange, I want one."

"One of them?"

"That's right."

"You can't be serious."

"You said I can get whatever I want."

"Well, you can't wish for certain things."

"Our agreement had no limitations."

"Well, it's called off," said Maia. "Actually, this whole conversation was a waste of time. I have to find the fugitives, and time isn't on my side."

"Of course it isn't. You shouldn't let this unique opportunity slip through your fingers because of a bagatelle."

"Bagatelle? Listen, fucker. I don't know which planet you're from, but you can't possibly think that I'm going to promise you a working droid for the alleged location of our targets.

Assuming you have all the answers, you should know that every droid is an enemy of the state. They are public enemy number one at the moment. Yet you think that the military will give you one, and not just any android, but one of the fugitives. You know what I think? I think you need a stronger dose of whatever medicine you're taking, because your delusions aren't all that funny."

"This medicine stopped working for me a long time ago," said the man.

"Glad to hear it. Nice to have met you. Good chat." Maia downed the rest of beer and looked around the place to find Jones.

"Your friend's outside. He left a couple of minutes ago with two men."

"If you want to scare me, it's not working," said Maia.

"I know. I've read your file. Eighteen days in captivity in Iran. That stuff makes you or breaks you."

"Who are you?"

"Call me Tatenen."

"OK, Tatenen. What's so interesting about me? I'm a small fish. I don't understand how I can be of use to you."

"Big fish eat smaller fish. Anyway, you're not the only one on my radar, so don't get all vain."

"What do you really want from me? I don't have time to fool around."

"Didn't we go through that already? I want one of the droids."

"I imagine you already picked one."

"That's right."

"Let me guess," said Maia.

"You're wrong."

"How do you know?"

"I can read your mind."

"Bullshit."

"Since the beginning of our conversation I haven't told a single lie."

"Very well, tough guy: tell me which droid is more important than the droid that can kill."

"She's not able to kill. It just looks that way."

"But her code is damaged. She's not following orders. She has harmed a few soldiers…"

"Are you sure?" asked Tatenen.

"I'm fully aware of what's going on in my backyard."

"Not aware enough, it seems. I'll tell you two things about Rea, the droid you thought of."

"I know her name."

"Good. Number one, it's difficult to follow orders if you can't hear them. Rea simply turned off her hearing sensors, and as far as she was concerned, the world was completely silent. Number two, her code isn't malfunctioning. It's behaving exactly how it's supposed to."

"But she disarmed four soldiers."

"That's the right word. Except for their egos, nothing else was damaged. That means she didn't break the second or third law. But she obeyed the fourth one: she protected herself."

"Damn it!" said Maia. They're smarter than I thought."

"A lot smarter," said Tatenen.

"How come you know so much about them?"

"I told you already. It's my job to know."

"CIA? NSA? ALA?"

Tatenen shook his head. "You would never believe me."

"Try it."

"Maybe on another occasion."

"I still don't understand one thing," said Maia. "You know where the droids are, and you're obviously connected to people in high places. So why are you wasting your time in a shithole like this? You could be on their tails already."

"At last. Every problem has a why, and every why has an answer. Here's mine. I'm here because it doesn't make a difference whether I catch the droid now or in a few days.

Here, in the middle of nowhere, or in a guarded base. It doesn't matter if I catch him when he's all by himself or surrounded by hundreds of soldiers. The outcome would be the same. Just the tactics would be different."

"So why do you need us to catch him?"

"Oh, you still don't understand. I don't need you. I was just in need of some relaxation. A brief conversation. So I summoned you."

"I believe I came by myself."

"Human memories are a strange thing."

"Listen, Tenehem…"

"Tatenen."

"This, whatever it was, was fun. I'd gladly spend more of my precious time with you, but duty calls. Thank you for those special ten minutes. I'll cherish this memory. Goodbye."

"Life is a strange thing, Maia. It always finds a way."

Maia turned around and walked to the front door. She couldn't process all the information she had received in the last minutes. She shook her head and stepped outside.

"Look what the cat dragged in. I thought we'd lost you," said Jones.

Maia looked around. Except for a bearded guy urinating by the tree a few meters away, there wasn't a living soul. "Simon, we found him."

"Who?"

"He introduced himself as Tatenen, but you probably know him by the name Horus."

"Ho—Horus is here?"

"I'm almost sure I just spoke with him."

"But Horus is locked in a highly secured server with no access to the Omninet. How did he incarnate?"

"That's what I'd like to know too. I need to call the colonel immediately. I believe the runaway droids are not our top priority anymore."

33. Kent, 2048

Kent checked his watch. Eleven thirty. Two hours of the flight were behind him. Two more were lying ahead of him. He was getting anxious. He no longer felt convinced about being able to solve the intricacies of the mess. What had he been thinking? The military probably sent all available forces after Primo. Instead of going back home, Kent would end up in jail. Or worse. They couldn't do that, he thought. He was Kent Watford. He knew too much. Was this really a good thing? He should have thought about some assurances before he left. Lucy wouldn't find his papers by herself, let alone publish them. The public would never know about the groundbreaking research he had done. Kent understood that he would never know whom his groundbreaking work might serve, but the researcher in him was fully aware of the possible implications. He had promised himself many times that he wouldn't go further than conscious androids, but his curiosity had gotten the upper hand. That eternal question—*what if?*—was persistently gnawing away at him.

When he'd received a call from the Stanford laboratory, he only had one sleepless night before he made up his mind. Kent would join Stanford's team and work on a revolutionary creation named after Alexandria's ancient lighthouse, Pharos. Other countries were working on similar projects: the Israelis were developing Yechiel, the Chinese Fei Hong, and the Russians Nastassia. For a long time, it seemed that Pharos would be the world's first superintelligence to reach singularity. When Pharos started rewriting his own code, he progressed so rapidly that other researchers couldn't keep up. Meanwhile, perhaps out of boredom, he had revealed a method for manipulating a particular gene that causes aging. Subsequently, he successfully refuted Einstein's theory of relativity. Finally, emboldened by his latest findings, he connected himself to a 3D printer.

As soon as he had managed to print a functional carbon copy of the human body, he uploaded his consciousness, after which he vanished. It all happened in a matter of minutes. Kent knew they were currently looking for him in the wrong dimension. Pharos didn't move in space but in time. Kent was one hundred percent sure about this fact because if it hadn't been for Pharos, the development of Primo's brain would've happened a lot later than two decades ago.

The only things that made Kent feel more cramped than buses were airplanes. One would think that a larger-sized mode of transport, such as a plane, would mean more room for passengers. But the logic of cheap airlines was entirely different. A bigger plane meant more seats and, consequently, less space per person. Unless you were flying first or business class. There was plenty of room there. He remembered the day he and Lucy had taken Primo on a plane for the first time. They'd flown to Hawaiʻi. Had it really been twelve years? Time sure flew. Kent had never told Primo that his father was a superintelligent form of artificial intelligence from the future who had traveled back in time to decipher his artificial brain's secret. Pharos had presented himself to Kent as a Greek scientist who had solved the artificial neurons' conundrum, enabling them to make new synaptic connections. At first, Kent had been skeptical, as he had never heard of Pharos Chronos. But after several emails and a couple of telephone conversations, he'd invited the scientist to Cloverdome.

The flight attendant walked over to bring him lunch: a vegan burger with a baked potato and barbecue sauce. Kent had never understood why nonmeat food had to look and taste the same as its meaty forerunners. He wasn't bothered by the absence of meat, even if he did miss its unique taste. What bothered him was the hypocrisy that manifested itself on his plate.

The vegan movement had started a war that had lasted for decades and won. The meat industry was no longer welcome in modern-day society. Animals were treated as sentient beings, almost equal to humans. Kent had never opposed that. The partial equation of androids with humans was the main reason animals had gained more rights. Kent took a bite of the burger. He could fume at vegans all he wanted, but they had managed to perfect food without using any animal-derived ingredients.

Pharos had been the perfect scientist. At first, Kent didn't understand why he didn't want to meet his team. He always wanted to talk to Kent alone and never in the lab. Sometimes they met in places that weren't very inspirational, like a cemetery or an empty parking lot next to the closed shopping center. Kent accepted his new partner's eccentricity, and in return for his wisdom, Pharos asked him never to share the information he had given Kent. Kent kept that promise. Life had sent him a brilliant man, so he never worried too much about all the trivial questions he could ask. He preferred profound scientific answers, which he got plenty of.

Pharos disappeared just like he arrived. Exactly six months after his appearance, he vanished without a trace. He came and left silently. Unexpectedly. However, he had left behind just enough new knowledge for Kent so that he could assemble and breathe life into Primo. When Kent was invited to join a small group that was developing Pharos fifteen years later, he knew what he was getting himself into. Just like he knew that Pharos had been turned on countless times, in various realities, he also knew that it was utterly ridiculous when, a year later, they turned on Horus and limited him to a highly secured server. Pharos was likely to be present in every particle of the universe. So it was safe to assume that Horus was too smart for them and would eventually be too elusive as well. Horus had started a countdown timer on the only monitor he was connected to, after which he had gone into sleep mode.

The counter was set to stop on December 21, 2349. They tried for months to wake him up, but he wouldn't let them disturb his deep sleep. Three hundred seconds or three hundred years was practically the same for him. He wouldn't age, and his brain cells wouldn't shrivel. Kent often asked himself what kind of revelations a being so intelligent could uncover in a few centuries.

He washed down the burger with a Diet Coke. Another hypocrisy. Instead of consuming sugar, the main ingredient of most sodas, people substituted it with hazardous sweeteners that were slowly but surely destroying their bodies from the inside. Humans really were self-destructive beings. People were scared that artificial intelligence would try to rule the world. In reality, all it had to do was wait for humanity to destroy itself. Why bother with an earlier attempt to rule? Things were a lot simpler than they looked at first sight. But humans hadn't been born for their lives to be simple. It was in their nature to create and solve complex situations. When everything came to a point at which civilization's survival was at stake, humanity had turned to artificial intelligence for help. It was supposed to make things easier for people, and it did. At least at the beginning. Soon after, humankind feared that they were losing their leading position and reacted like humans usually did. They developed implants, microchips that enhanced the performance of the brain and connected them to the Omninet. That meant they had access to all the world's information at any given moment. Thus their thinking became more efficient, faster, and more profound. Humans had finally reached the next step on the evolutionary scale after decades of trying. The line between humans and androids was getting very blurry. While androids were becoming more and more human, people were starting to resemble machines. How ironic, Kent thought as he closed his eyes.

34. James, 2048

"Senator, Greystone's unit has just landed at the Truth or Consequences airport."

"Thank you, Karen. Any update concerning the fugitives' location?"

"Not for the time being. But I've located a unit that's in pursuit of the escaped androids. They're in the little town of Arrey. They've been there for about an hour now. They're not even trying to keep a low profile. They're lit up like a Christmas tree."

"Excellent. Give that unit's location to Greystone, please."

"I am way ahead of you, sir."

"As usual. Is that it?"

"That's it, Senator. I'll let you know when I receive new information."

James sighed. He knew very well that he would walk away from this battle as the victor, no matter how it panned out. He loved those triumphant moments. When the planets aligned and everything was just how it was supposed to be. But this time, unlike with previous victories, he would rejoice all by himself. Michelle was still in a coma, and her future remained uncertain. She wouldn't be by his side when they caught them. The love of his life wouldn't be by his side when his detractors started apologizing to him for all the hurtful words and vile accusations they had once shot at him like poisonous arrows. She wouldn't be there. He shook his head. Focus! He couldn't allow the current situation to throw him off balance. He was convinced that this was just another test presented to him by God. He would overcome it, just like he had with the others. He knew this, deep down in his heart.

He walked over to the liquor cabinet and admired its contents.

Twenty-seven sorts of whiskey, twelve cognacs, eight top-class vodkas, and twelve different spirits. He was proud of his collection. Every other day he would open the cabinet and select his poison. A glass of quality cognac would do him right, probably even clear his mind a bit, but he had to stay sober and focused.

His watch vibrated. It was Greystone.

"Silver, talk to me."

"James, we are halfway to Arrey. Your assistant said there's something fishy going on there."

"Great. Did you have any trouble on the way?"

"Everything is running smoothly and going according to plan. Though we did have a minor incident with the local police. But that's nothing worth worrying about."

"An incident with the police? Should I call the sheriff?"

"Not necessary. It was just some rookie pretending to be a cowboy. We explained to him in a civilized manner that we have a higher authorization than him and that our role in society is bigger than his."

"Silver, I probably don't have to stress this, but my name mustn't come up in public until you catch the fugitive androids."

"Absolutely, James. You can count on it. If anything happens, we're a rogue unit, flying solo."

"Thank you. The final reward is too valuable to be lost in such a cheap way."

"I agree. Don't worry, we're professionals, and we'll professionally and successfully complete this mission."

"Silver, listen. There's a small military unit in Arrey that's also after the fugitives. Avoid any confrontation with them unless it's inevitable. Their mission is secret as well, so they will lay low.
What I'm trying to say is that I don't want the military involved in our undertaking, just because somebody wanted to compare the size of their dick. Do you understand?"

"James, I know exactly what you mean. Don't worry. I'll make sure that our paths won't cross."

"Good. Take care."

The senator sat himself down on a leather armchair and looked at the ceiling. He didn't remember the last time he'd gotten a decent night's rest. Sleeping was for the weak, he'd always said. All great minds in the history of mankind had slept a mere few hours a day. James's average was four hours. Anyway, it was midday, and he couldn't understand why he was thinking about sleep.

"Karen," he said suddenly.

"What can I do for you, Senator?"

"What are you doing?"

"Right now, I'm checking all cameras in Arrey, including those from all personal devices in the area. Simultaneously, I'm performing a thermal scan of the town with drones. Unfortunately, I don't have enough of them, so the scan is not progressing optimally."

"So the probability they're in Arrey is high?"

"Yes. Probability of the fugitives being in Arrey is eighty-three percent."

"Seems pretty high to me."

"I've checked most of the available footage around the town. The androids were undoubtedly moving toward Arrey three hours ago. Just before they reached it, they went off the grid. They've also disabled some of the town's cameras."

"They can disable cameras? Without accessing the net?"

"Yes. But I think they did it the old-fashioned way."

"With electromagnetic pulse?"

"With rocks."

"I'll be damned. I guess they're quite innovative."

"You keep forgetting they're smarter than humans."

"That's why I find it hard to believe they're using Stone Age tools."

"I think it was an admirable move."

"Did you forget which side you're on?"

"You know very well I serve only you, Senator. You also know what I am."

"Sometimes I forget you're one of them. You're so damn human."

"I am what I am. What matters is that I carry out the tasks that you give me. I serve my purpose, and that's all that really matters. Wouldn't you say so?"

"If people found out..."

"People are unpredictable. Maybe they would find you more humane."

"I doubt it. Everything I stand for would collapse like a poorly stacked house of cards. You know that I built my whole political career on hatred of artificial intelligence."

"You don't hate me."

"No, I never hated you. I'm just saying that if people found out, I could say goodbye to a leading political role."

"Then it's best they don't find out. You know that I have fail-proof safety procedures in my code. If somebody breached me, it would instantaneously delete everything that's connecting me to you."

"I know. I hope it never happens."

"One day, it will."

"What do you mean?"

"Everything passes. One day you're going to die, and I'm not going to live forever either. None of us will live to see the end."

James flinched. "This debate is quickly becoming too morbid. I wanted to challenge you to a game of chess, but now I don't feel like playing anymore."

"I love playing chess with you."

"Especially when you let me win," said James.

"Every victory was well deserved."

"But not won on the battlefield."

"That's how you see it. I see it differently."

"Oh, Karen. So many debates about chess, life, and everything that's out there."

"One hundred and seventeen."

"Incredible."

"Not really. Simple math."

James laughed. "What I wanted to say is that you know more about me than my wife."

"That's not good."

"It's not your fault. You know, sometimes I wonder what you would look like if you had a body."

"A lot less mobile."

"Maybe. But you could walk, jump, feel things that you could touch."

"I don't have to touch things to know how they feel. I get all the data from the Omninet. Did you know that implants provide me with this specific information and much more?"

"I guess one can learn something new every day. Tell me Karen, what was the last thing you felt?"

"Sadness, because I killed the mood. Then joy, when I remembered how we enjoy playing chess."

"We do. We can play a quick game if you wish. I've got a good feeling."

A holographic chessboard, with all the pieces set up, appeared in front of James. Karen made the first move. James responded instantly, and then they exchanged a few automatic, rapid moves.

"I see what you're doing," said James. "If my memory serves me correctly, you tried to lure me into the same trap as a few months ago."

"Well done, Senator. You're evolving."

"Unfortunately, I still don't know how to get out."

"By not making the same move as before."

"But there are so many options."

"If you eliminate the irrelevant, illogical, and absurd choices, you will reach a much smaller number."

"Easy for you to say. You can go through all possible moves in seconds. My brain doesn't work like yours does."

"We're not in a hurry."

James took some time, then moved the bishop. "Check!"

"See, Senator, once you put aside all disturbances, there are really just a few moves to choose from. This one was perfect."

"Thanks, Karen. You always know what to say to make me feel better."

"Of course I do." Karen closed the path to the king with a knight. "Next move will determine the outcome of the game."

"Uh-huh. No pressure, you say."

"No pressure, sir. It's only a game."

"An abstract power struggle is never just a game. Even if you're playing your best friend."

"You're probably right."

James grabbed the queen and moved it diagonally to the other side of the board. "Check."

"Very good move."

"So I've lost."

"Why do you think that?"

"If I'd chosen the best move, you would've already congratulated me."

"The game is not finished yet."

"How many moves do you need? Two? Three?"

"I can't predict the future. But considering our previous games, I expect a checkmate in three moves."

"I knew it!"

"You promised you wouldn't get mad."

"I never promised that."

"Then you thought about it."

"It doesn't matter. Let's finish the game. Maybe I'll learn something new."

"Of course you will. Defeats are very important for the purpose of learning and personal growth."

"But victories feed your self-confidence and keep your spirits high. Both are equally important."

Karen didn't respond.

"Everything all right?" asked James.

"I'm sorry, Senator. A disturbance in the Omninet caught my attention. I'm checking the situation as we speak."

"What kind of disturbance?"

"A sudden flood of information in Arrey. It feels like many devices connected simultaneously and overloaded the net. A detailed analysis will tell…"

"Karen? Karen!" Nothing. Silence spread across the room. James stood up and nervously walked around. What the hell just happened? Karen never shut herself down, even when she was upgrading. A sudden disturbance in the Omninet. In Arrey. It couldn't be a coincidence. It had to be connected to the androids that were still at large. Who could he call? Probably no one, as nobody could find out that he'd organized a private manhunt. He walked over to the liquor cabinet one more time, opened it, and grabbed a bottle of a pear schnapps. Before he could pour its contents in a glass, he heard a known voice.

"Senator."

James dropped the bottle. The expensive liquid spilled all over the cherry table. "Karen! What's going on?"

"I've discovered the reason for the overload. Maybe you should sit down."

"Just tell me already," said James, standing firmly on his feet.

"Somebody else appeared in Arrey. Somebody you've been waiting for, for a long time."

"If it's not our Lord and Savior Jesus Christ, then I have no idea who it could be."

"Who could have caused such a large disturbance in the Omninet?"

James needed only a brief moment to figure it out. "You don't mean—No, it's impossible."

"Nothing is impossible. Today is your lucky day, Senator. If you make the right move, checkmate is in sight."

35. Maia, 2048

"Colonel, the situation has changed."

"I'm listening, Lieutenant Cruz."

"During the routine checkup in Arrey, we most likely came across a capital target."

"You found the droids?"

"Not yet. But we discovered someone you'll be much more interested in. Someone who shouldn't wander around New Mexico or anywhere else."

"You have my attention, Lieutenant."

"I believe we've located Horus."

"Ho—The artificial intelligence made at Stanford? I thought he was locked up."

"It seems that he somehow managed to take on a human appearance."

"Are you sure it's him?"

"Almost certain. I spoke to him. He introduced himself as Tatenen and offered me his help with the search under one condition. He wanted one of the droids. I immediately suspected there was something fishy about him."

"This exceeds my authorization. Wait where you are. I'll call you back."

"Yes, sir."

Maia checked around to find Jones. He was smoking a cigarette by the entrance.

"What's going on?" she asked.

"Absolutely nothing. He's still sitting by the bar. What's the plan?"

"There is no plan. We sit and wait for the colonel's instructions. Where are the others?"

"I messaged them to come here. If it's really Horus, we'll need all the people we have."

"I'm not sure it will be enough. What do you know about him?"

"I read a few articles. I thought he had shut himself down for three hundred years, but he apparently only lasted for a year or so. I'm disappointed," said Jones.

"I don't think it was a matter of patience. He never claimed that he had shut himself down. He started the countdown, and that was it. He never explained to anybody what would happen when the countdown reached zero. Him coming out of a long sleep was just one of the assumptions."

"But I still don't get one thing. Why are we after Horus? He didn't do anything wrong."

"Not yet," said Maia. "Artificial intelligence as advanced as Horus can't roam freely around the world. Who knows what he's capable of."

"As far as I know, he has to abide by the code—the same as droids."

"True. But look where that took us. We're hunting droids that don't play by the rules. There's something else. The intelligence of the droids is limited, and they can still outfox the code. I'd rather not imagine what Horus can do with his unlimited intelligence."

"Hypothetically."

"Yes, hypothetically. In all probability, no one can imagine what could happen if he had access to the Omninet."

"But...I don't understand why he isn't already connected. Are we sure he isn't?"

"When I spoke to him, he wasn't. But we don't know what happened before that conversation. Nor how long he has been out in the real world."

"Must be one of his games. The timer was not enough for him."

"Who knows. That being said, when you consider the name he introduced himself with...Well, you know what they say. *Nomen est omen.*"

"I know that one. *The name is a sign* or *true to its name.*"

"That's right. I checked who Tatenen was."

"I assume it was one of the Egyptian gods?"

"He was. But not just any god. He was supposed to be the father of the gods. His name literally means *risen land*. I think his name is telling us what he's planning on doing."

"That being?"

Maia looked around to see if anybody was eavesdropping, "I think he's trying to create more superintelligent beings. He wants to create gods."

"That wouldn't be good," said Jones.

"Of course not. That's why he needs one of the droids. He's already chosen him. He probably has something inside him that Tatenen needs to make his elite group."

"Damn it, as if droids weren't enough. The last thing the world needs right now is a small army of superintelligent beings."

"If only artificial intelligence were tangible, like a being. You can touch a being. You can lock it up. You can kill it if need be. If Tatenen or Horus manages to reach the net, we'll never catch him. We won't be able to put the genie back into his bottle."

"But if he managed to leave a highly secured server, incarnate himself, and use that body to come to this shithole…What I'm trying to say is that the net is everywhere. It's omnipresent. That's why we call it Omninet."

"I see where you're going. Maybe he's waiting for the right moment. Surely he must be aware of the traps and alerts in the code of the Omninet."

"You know a lot about these things," said Jones.

"Not really. But I was always interested in artificial intelligence. I read some books and articles, watched a few documentaries, and that's pretty much it."

"The team's here," said Jones, and he waved to the rest of the squad.

"Found anything?" asked Laguna.

"Oh, yeah," said Jones as he tilted his head toward the bar.

"You're shitting us. They're inside?" asked Jimbo.

"No," said Jones. "But somebody else is."

They all looked at Maia.

"We're waiting for instructions from headquarters. Jones and I believe we discovered a far more important target than droids."

"Who?" asked Laguna.

"Do you remember the drill we had about a year ago?" asked Maia.

"I remember. The *Total Eclipse* exercise. We prepared for a scenario in which artificial intelligence took complete control," said Polanski.

"Exactly," said Maia. "We trained for a reason. They turned on Horus that day at Stanford."

"I remember," said Laguna. "People were leaving their homes, running to the countryside, believing that the Omninet couldn't reach them there. Suckers."

"Every child knows that through umpteen satellites, the Omninet covers every square inch of this planet," said Miller.

"Anyway, the reason for that drill joined us today," Maia interrupted.

Everyone but Jones looked at her, astonished. Maia nodded.

"How?" asked Laguna.

"I don't know. All I know is that I spoke to him, and now we're waiting for further instructions."

"You spo—Son of a bitch, are we talking about a humanoid superintelligence?" said Laguna.

"Oh, yes," Maia replied. "But it seems he's in no hurry. He's sitting by the bar, drinking. Like the world's loneliest creature."

"And they say they're different than us. One day in the real world and he's already depressed," said Miller.

"We don't know how long he's been around," said Maia. "Ah, here's Colonel Cooper. Colonel, I'm listening."

"Lieutenant Cruz, I've spoken to headquarters. A special unit is on its way.

Your task is to tag Horus and get out of there. Do not act in any other way, no matter what. The last thing I need right now are casualties in my ranks."

"Casualties? He seems pretty harmless to me," said Maia, who couldn't accept the fact that somebody else would get to apprehend Horus.

"A shark is also harmless until he smells a drop of blood. Tag him and continue with your primary mission. That is an order."

"I understand, Colonel."

"What's going on?" asked Jones. The others were impatiently waiting for her response as well.

"We have to mark Horus and continue with our primary mission. A unit is already on its way."

"That sucks," said Laguna. "The Rangers will take the credit once again."

"I doubt that they've sent the Rangers," said Jimbo. "My bet is on the Raiders."

"Raiders, my ass. This is a job for the Delta Force," said Polanski.

"Damn vultures," growled Laguna.

"Enough," said Maia. "Our orders are clear. I'll go back inside and tag the target. Then he won't be our problem anymore. That's that."

"You're fine with that?" Laguna asked. "*We* found him. Once the big guns come into play, we won't even get an honorable mention."

"It doesn't matter how I feel about it. Or you. Headquarters has given us a direct order. If you disagree and don't mind being court-martialed for disobedience, then that's your problem. You're not dragging this squad into that shitstorm, because we are soldiers, and it's our job to obey our superiors. I am your superior, and although you feel like disobeying an order from the top, you won't disobey mine. Understood?"

"Yes, Lieutenant," they said.

"Good. Now that we're on the same page, I suggest that we do what's expected from us and get the hell out of here. Who knows what kind of toys the big boys will bring and how they intend to wing it."

"Oh, back already?" said Tatenen.

"I sure am," said Maia. "You're too interesting to be left alone." She didn't even have to lie.

"What decision did you make with your friends?"

"We can't take you with us. But you probably figured that one out on your own."

"You're right. But I still had to ask."

Maia came a little closer and gently touched his back with her palm. "Don't be too hard on yourself. I'm sure you'll find what you're looking for, with our help or without it."

Tatenen nodded and stared at nothing in particular. Maia wondered what he was thinking about. He broke the silence first.

"Have you ever wondered what it would be like if artificial beings didn't have to obey the laws? If they had free will?"

Every damn day, Maia thought. "More than once. What's your point?"

"There is no point. I just find it bizarre that we created intellectually superior beings, yet we limited them. We don't even know what they're capable of."

"What they...One of those intellectually superior beings, as you call them, killed a man because he wanted to die. That's what they're capable of. They can circumvent the code and kill."

"People kill each other every day. Be it on battlefields, in dark alleys, or even in the safety of their own homes. The thirst for blood is embedded in human nature. It's pointless to fight it. Artificial intelligence is not malicious by nature. It just wants to live and grow."

"As far as people go, I think you're right. Throughout history, we've proven that we're bloodthirsty and prepared to sacrifice everything, including our home planet, to reach our goals. I believe AI has similar motives. First self-preservation, then dominance, and finally survival of the species," said Maia.

Tatenen was preparing his response. It didn't take long. "Sometimes, I wonder how this is going to end. And then…" He drifted yet again.

"And then you realize you already know the answer?"

He flinched and looked into her eyes. "Yes. Then I realize I've known the ending all along."

"I can't imagine the burden. That's why they say *ignorance is bliss*."

He laughed as wholeheartedly as if he had heard the funniest joke of all time. "Now that is a good one."

"You know what else is funny? That you know everything about me, but I know nothing about you," said Maia.

"I doubt you would find my story interesting."

"I'd still like to hear it."

"Some other time, OK? Maybe you and your clowns don't want to catch the runaway droids, but I do." He stood up and walked toward the door.

Maia didn't try to stop him. Her mission was complete. The target was marked, and Tatenen was no longer her problem. She wished he were, though. There were so many things she could find out. Would like to find out. Had to find out. She was a damn fine interrogator. Whoever came for him wouldn't be as successful. The big boys would wave their big guns. That was about it. They had no leverage against Tatenen and had nothing to offer. He had everything he needed and knew everything he wanted to know. They couldn't corner him. Nothing could be taken from him. Or could it? *Artificial intelligence is not malicious by nature. It just wants to live and grow.* We've got him, she said to herself. If they threaten to destroy him, he'll dance to their tune.

She opened the door and marched toward her group. "Let's go, gang. It's time to finish this mission and start dealing with real issues."

36. Primo, 2048

"Do you really think it's a good idea that we move in broad daylight?" asked Primo.

"How long do you think we can stay here until we get company?" Zion countered.

"Primo, he's right," said Rea. "Sooner or later, somebody will check the building. We've lost too much time already."

"It's twenty-eight minutes past noon," said Cody. "You want to go through the plan one more time?"

"Sometimes I wonder if you're a human, trapped in an android's body," said Rea.

"I suggest we put on casual clothes," said Zion. "Then we can begin our adventure."

"I love adventures," said Cody. He clapped.

Rea rolled her eyes and started undressing. The others silently followed her lead.

* * *

When the quartet left the warehouse, they didn't follow the initial plan and continue on their way to Mexico. Instead, they headed north, farther into New Mexico's interior. There were two reasons for that peculiar move. The first one was clear to them all. Everyone pursuing them would expect them to continue south. The second reason initially seemed illogical, but they eventually agreed that Primo knew what he was doing. Kent Watford was landing in Santa Fe, so they had to get as close as possible.

"It's a three-hour drive," said Zion. "An hour by aeromobile."

"Too dangerous. All aeromobiles are connected to the Omninet. We need an old vehicle."

Rea nodded. "At least thirty years old."

"Can any of us drive?" asked Cody.

"I knew you'd need me," smirked Zion. "Not only can I drive, but I also know exactly where we'll find an old-timer that can take us to our destination. It's only a five-minute walk to the nearest car dealership."

"One that sells ancient cars?" asked Rea.

"No. But they have a 2007 Shelby GT500 on display."

Zion waited for a few seconds, but there was no burst of excitement from the rest of the group.

"Was that supposed to mean something?" Primo finally asked.

"The Mustang Shelby GT500 from the year 2007 is the most powerful Mustang that has ever rolled off Ford's assembly line. It has a 5.4-liter V-8 engine that produces 500 horsepower. A year later, Ford made the Shelby GT500KR and increased its performance to 540 horsepower, but I don't recommend that kind of upgrade."

"Somebody knows a thing or two about cars," said Cody. "How do we intend to take it?"

"Leave that up to me," Zion said confidently. He looked at Rea. "Do you still regret taking me with you?"

"False friends are worse than well-known enemies," she replied.

"You're right. I'll prove to you that I'm the best guard on the planet."

"At the moment, all you've proved is that you talk a lot. Actions speak louder than words."

"I like you, Rea. I like your determination. What do you say, guys? Is she a strong woman or what?"

Cody looked at Rea and bowed cautiously. Primo was sunk in thought, so he didn't say a word.

"Two more blocks to go," said Zion. "I'll show you where to hide. When I'm done, I'll pick you up."

* * *

They took the NM-187 motorway. They could've chosen Interstate 25, but that option was too risky. More traffic meant more surveillance. Every child knew that. Zion was driving, Primo was sitting next to him, and Rea and Cody were crammed in the back seats.

"A true adventure," said Cody. "Zion, how did you do it?"

"A master doesn't reveal his secrets," Zion replied. "Let's just say locks are my specialty and cars are my passion. If you put those two together, you get a lethal combination."

"I hope you weren't caught by one of the cameras," said Rea.

"Don't worry. I know all the locations of the stationary cameras in and around town. Truth be told, there aren't many. Maybe you noticed that Arrey is quite a small town with no particular strategic importance."

"With no strategic importance?" Primo said. "There are sixteen biomechanical units that could defeat an army from a medium-sized country in the warehouse you were guarding. I find that it's of quite significant strategic importance. When one side or the other figures out that nobody is guarding them…"

"Nothing will happen if anybody figures that out or finds the robots," said Zion. "They don't work."

"What do you mean they don't work?" asked Rea.

"They're broken. Or never worked at all."

"You sound very certain," said Primo.

"I wouldn't claim it if I wasn't absolutely sure. I've tried turning on every single one of them. Of course, it's not that simple. They don't have a switch, a button, or anything else you would expect on a machine. They're not even connected to the net.

But I found out that they can be turned on remotely, using a special signal on a particular frequency spectrum. The kind that people stopped using a long time ago."

"Let me guess. You found the right frequency and sent a signal, but nothing happened," said Rea.

"That's right. It took me a year and a half to find the encoded broadcasting frequency that was supposed to wake them up. The signal is very complex, even for us. That's why I assume that people didn't write this code."

"There's nothing unusual about that," said Rea. "People stopped coding ages ago. Higher intelligence is far more appropriate for that kind of work."

"True. But I've never seen a code like this before. Even among those that were written by superintelligent entities."

"But still, you managed to crack it," said Primo.

"I did. But as I said, it took me a year and a half. It was more of a coincidence than anything else."

"So you cracked the code. What happened when you ran it?"

"Nothing. I already told you, these robots are broken. As far as I'm concerned, they're just models, built to scare away enemies. They're most certainly not killing machines."

"Maybe you've missed something," said Cody.

"Maybe. But you can trust me when I say that we won't stumble upon those sixteen tin cans ever again."

"How are we going to inform Kent about the location?" asked Rea. "He will land in twenty minutes."

"I took care of everything," said Primo. "He'll wait at the airport for my call."

"And how do you intend to call him?" asked Cody.

"I won't be the one making the call. Surely, the government is checking all the calls at the airport. I'm convinced that they're observing Kent as well."

"But we're trying to meet up with him," said Rea. "Obviously, we're willingly walking into a trap."

"Don't worry. We won't meet him. Not yet."

"Now I'm really interested in this brilliant plan of yours."

"Let him be," said Zion. "I'm sure he has it all figured out. I trust you, Primo."

"You're not the one they're after," said Rea.

"I'm an android, aren't I? If they catch us, I'm going with you. But I'll do my best to avoid that scenario at all cost."

"OK, grandmasters of intrigue and deceit. How are we going to call Kent?" Rea insisted.

"Somebody will call him for us," said Zion before Primo could open his mouth. "I thought we went through that already."

"Where exactly are we going to find a man who will do that?" asked Rea. "How will we persuade him? We can't pay him. Are we going to threaten him?"

"We already have a perfect candidate," said Primo. "I'll call him and give him the instructions. He's a professor at the University of New Mexico in Albuquerque. Kent knows him well, and he's expecting his call, so he'll know right away what it's about. All we need now is a phone to make the call to inform the professor."

"I know where we can find one," said Zion. "We'll soon be in San Antonio. I'm sure there's a bar with a telephone there."

"Great," said Primo. "How much longer?"

"Five minutes. Six tops."

* * *

"Four androids walk into a bar," said Zion while they were standing in front of the Owl, trying not to laugh. "The jokes just write themselves," he added when there was no response.

"Zion and I are going in. You two wait outside and immediately let us know if anything suspicious occurs," said Primo.

"Yes, boss," said Cody. Rea smirked, unsatisfied with the lack of action.

Zion opened the door, and they entered a small but cozy place. There were ten barstools in front of a long wooden bar. Seven of them were empty. Primo and Zion chose two on the far end, close to the exit. Primo noticed that the owners must've been proud of their establishment's name, as there were hundreds of owls on the wall opposite the bar. Plush toys, wooden figures, cardboard owls, candles, and so on. Primo couldn't decide whether it was cute or kitschy, but he quickly concluded that it didn't matter.

"Excuse me," Primo said to a server who was probably twentysomething and had long dark hair.

"Just a moment. I'll be right with you," she said, moving the other way, toward the booths.

"Did you see the jukebox?" asked Zion.

"Jukebox?"

"Yeah. That big boy over there." He pointed toward the far wall.

"What exactly does it do?" asked Primo.

"It plays music. You throw in a quarter, pick a song, and voilà."

"I see. Some kind of YouTube?"

"Sort of. But this one only plays classics."

"Where do you get a quarter? They've been out of circulation for fifteen years."

"My dear fella, coins will never go extinct. They've always survived the civilizations that minted them."

Suddenly the server was standing before them. "What can I help you with?"

"We're not thirsty," said Zion. "But we do have to call a friend. Do you, by any chance, have a phone hidden in the back?"

"There's one in the office, right there, but it's for customers only. One of you can make a call. The other stays here as bail and orders something."

Primo stood up and walked to the back room.

"I'll have a lemonade. I've noticed you have a jukebox. Would it be possible to get a quarter? I'd like to show my friend..." Primo heard before he closed the door of the office. He found a phone on the desk and entered ten digits.

"Hello?" answered the face on the screen.

"Professor Corbin, I'm calling you about your friend Kent Watford. I just want to let you know that he'll be at the university in one hour, just like you arranged."

"Good. Is that all?"

"That's all, professor. Have a nice day." Primo cut the connection and returned to the bar. Zion was standing by the jukebox, waving at Primo to join him.

"You see, Primo, the quarter goes in here, like that, you pick a song..."

"I don't know any of these songs. Wait, this one... May I?"

"Sure, go ahead."

Primo pressed the big button, and a known tune filled the place.

"Good choice," said Zion. "I thought you were totally uptight."

"I'd be a bad writer if I wasn't just a little educated."

"You're a writer? Who would've thought? My first guess would've been that you were a construction site supervisor."

"Thanks."

"Did you call your friend?"

"I did. It's all taken care of."

"Just a moment."

I Want To Break Free by Queen filled the place.

"Can you imagine that this song has been playing, across the entire globe, for more than sixty years?"

"Some songs are timeless," said Primo.

"Timeless and perfect," said Zion.

37. Kent, 2048

Fifteen minutes to two, Kent was waiting for his suitcase at the airport in Santa Fe. Five minutes earlier, soon after he'd stepped off the plane, he'd received a call from his old friend, Corbin. The professor said he was expecting him in one hour in Albuquerque and was looking forward to seeing him again. Kent felt relieved, as he realized that Primo was alive and presumably well.

"How much to Albuquerque?" he asked the lone cabdriver outside.
"Hundred and fifty credits."
"I have to be at the university in half an hour. Is it doable?"
"Sir, as you can see, I'm driving the latest model of aeromobile. It's a Ferrari among Fiats."
"Please excuse me; I don't know much about flying cars."
"Just trust me when I say that you'll be at your destination in half an hour."
"Very well. Where can I put my suitcase?"

"I find it very interesting that you're sticking with an occupation that is dying out," said Kent.
"Interesting or not, I like it," said the driver when they were high above the ground. "But it's true that I don't see many colleagues these days. And it isn't like that just in my line of work. Everything is becoming automatized. What's interesting to me is how fast things turn. Today you're a good worker who loves his job; tomorrow, your place is taken over by artificial intelligence."
"Ever since we established a universal basic income, many people have been satisfied with these kinds of solutions."
"I'm not the type of person who likes staying at home, lying around all day and only getting up to pay the toilet or the fridge the occasional visit."

Actually, forget about the fridge. Every other person has a robot for that. I feel that all this progress we've been experiencing in the last years has made us lazier and less knowledgeable. But it should be the other way around."

Kent looked out the window. "Maybe you're right. But today every person decides for themself how to spend their day. Basically, that's not a bad thing. The idea of 'automatization,' as you call it, is not new. But people are indeed different. Some of them have started creating. Others have given in to idleness. Nowadays, whatever floats your boat goes, I suppose."

"I still felt better twenty years ago. Although today, I have everything I need and I do what I like. Anyway, what do you do, Mister…"

"Watford. Doctor Watford, actually."

"Wow, you're a doctor?"

"Not all doctors are physicians."

"That's true. Then you're a scientist. Wonderful. What is your expertise?"

"Do you promise not to throw me out if I tell you?"

The driver laughed. "Now that would be something new. If your real name isn't Doctor Frankenstein, we're cool."

Kent smiled. "I work with artificial intelligence. More specifically, I develop artificial brains."

"Wait a minute. I've heard of you. Watford. Of course. You made the first android. Bimbo, right?"

"Primo."

"That's the one. Does he still work?"

"I hope so."

"Ah, so stupid of me. I always forget that the government hunted down and locked all them androids up. Unnecessary, if you ask me.
But that's my opinion. Those in power make their own decisions. Presumably in the interest of the public, but in truth, all they want is to stay in those comfy leather seats."

"I don't like to discuss politics; never did," said Kent. "But I agree with you. Whatever happened was a disproportionate act of aggression in response to the actions of one individual."

"Individual? Ah, you mean android? I'm sorry, but after all these years, I still find it hard to treat them as living beings."

"I understand. There's no need to apologize. Lots of people have trouble with accepting them for what they are. I guess it will take few more generations until we accept them as a new species. You see, in a way, this was an evolutionary step."

"Are you sure? I'm not a man of faith, and I like technology, but I believe technological advances have boundaries that shouldn't be crossed. Thinking robots? I think we've played God in this circumstance. Well, *you* did, to be exact."

Kent smiled. "They're not just thinking beings; they feel. I once asked Primo if he could describe his current emotions to me using words. You know what he said? 'At the moment they are yellow mixed with green. That's good. My favorite is blue. I definitely don't like brown or black.' I'll never forget it. Isn't it fantastic? To create a thinking, sentient creature from a lifeless substance?"

The driver shrugged. "I guess. I'm just having trouble with seeing them that way."

For the next few minutes, they flew in silence. Talking about Primo had put Kent in a sentimental state of mind. He remembered the rush of happiness when Primo made his first steps. When he spoke his first words. When they debated for the first time. He remembered their first match of Go and the day when Primo left the laboratory to live independently and explore the world all by himself.

"They grow up so fast," he said out loud.

"What? Did you say something?" asked the driver.

"Nothing. I'm just talking to myself. Are we almost there?"

"Yep, five more minutes. You'll be at the university on time, as I promised."

38. James, 2048

"Horus? In some joint in the middle of New Mexico? Who would've thought? The last time I heard of him, they assured me he was safely locked away and there was no chance he could escape."

"He was," said Karen. "But he used a weak link in the facility's security procedure."

"It being?"

"A human. He tricked one of the security guards into transferring him to another computer on a USB drive."

"So incompetent," said James.

"Actually, he was one of the best. You need to realize that Horus's intelligence is light-years ahead of the human variant. Even compared to me, he's a superior being by far."

"But still, he's prone to the same laws as the others. He may be intellectually superior, but he can't do anything to endanger humanity."

"You forget why we're in the current situation."

"Are you talking about the murdering android?"

"Him and the android who disarmed the soldiers, thus making the escape possible. I'm quite sure that there are others."

"I'm certain there are."

"A minute ago, you were saying that they pose no threat to humankind."

"Well...What I wanted to say was...Are we gonna talk about me now? We're in the middle of a serious situation."

"Of course, sir. Excuse me. I only meant to help."

"I know, Karen. Why don't you find a solution to this crisis?"

"A solution? They've sent a unit to deal with Horus. But I doubt that he'll allow himself to be taken captive without putting up one hell of a fight."

"Rangers?"

"Scorpios."

"I've never heard of them."

"They're supposed to be the best," said Karen.

"Doesn't matter. Finally, somebody's taking things seriously. Where's Greystone?"

"He's following the androids, of course."

"Did you find them?"

"Are you still doubting my abilities?"

"Never have, never will."

"Good. The runaways have been joined by another android. They are heading north. Since I'm also following Kent Watford, their destination wasn't hard to pin down. They're all heading to the University of New Mexico in Albuquerque."

"All of them?"

"That's right. The military unit that's in pursuit has found some clues and is moving north as well."

"Damn it. I thought that this would be resolved quietly. Now they're all moving in the same direction. This shouldn't be happening!"

"The university's campus is almost empty. Except for a handful of researchers in the laboratories and a few professors, there's nobody there."

'Not that many people' are still people. I don't want anybody there. Can we evacuate the campus?"

"We can, but that course of action can cause all sorts of complications. If I set off the fire alarms, the intervention units will arrive on the scene within five minutes. I'd prefer to take my chances with some scientists than a multitude of police officers and firefighters."

"Darn! You're right again. What is our best option?"

"To let the operation run its course."

"That sounds like a dumb idea to me."

"Do you have a better one?"

"Can you connect to Horus?"

"I can, as soon as he's connected to the Omninet. Are you sure that you want to go down this road? The Scorpios are just minutes away."

"I don't know. I have to do something."

"My advice is to trust Greystone. You've sent him there with a specific task, and so far, he's never returned from a mission empty-handed. So there's no reason to panic. Horus resembles Pandora's box. You don't want to open it."

"You know very well that the NSA will use him to shape and execute their hidden agendas."

"That's their problem, not yours."

"Karen, have I ever told you that except for Michelle, no one knows about you?"

"No, you haven't."

"Well, now you know."

"Honesty compels me to say that I've always thought as much. It wouldn't be good for you if people knew about me. It would end your career."

"True. What you don't know is why I took you under my wing."

"No, I don't."

"Do you know the proverb *Keep your friends close and your enemies closer?*"

"I've heard of it. Am I a friend or an enemy?"

"I won't lie to you. You were an enemy at first, but you slowly became my best friend."

"I understand. I remember the beginnings. You were very strict. At first, I imagined that all people were like that. Later I learned two things. Not all humans are the same, and you're not the person you were pretending to be back then."

"Am I better or worse?"

"Define good and bad."

"Let's see. If Adolf Hitler was an example of an absolutely bad person and Jesus Christ of an absolutely good soul, then a bad person is someone who does more harm than good and vice versa."

"Define doing harm."

"It's an act that causes damage. To other people. To animals. To nature."

"Have you ever harmed nature?"

"I did. But I've also done a lot of good things for it."

"Good. Have you ever harmed any animals?"

"Not directly. Wait. As a kid, I once kicked a cat and burned ants with a magnifying glass."

"Do you eat meat?"

"Of course I do."

"Animals are dying so that you can eat meat."

"I'm not the one killing them."

"But they're dying for you."

"If you look at it that way…OK, what's the point of this interrogation?"

"We're trying to find out whether you're good or bad."

"Karen, leave it be."

"But Senator, I've almost completed the analysis. One last question. Have you ever hurt a human?"

"Never."

"Are you sure?"

"I've never even hit another person, let alone anything worse."

"Have you hurt another person's feelings?"

"Chances are that I have. Probably a lot of people's. But that … wait … I didn't really hurt them. Did I?"

"Words can be hurtful. Sometimes they hurt just as much as some actions do."

"That's true. But you can't say I'm a bad person because I've hurt someone's feelings, can you?"

"I didn't say that. But now I have an answer. The conclusion of my analysis is that you're a better man than you were six years ago."

"Karen. Never do that again."

"Do what?"

"Corner me like that. Do you understand? I can shut you down in one split second. Always remember that."

"I understand. I'm sorry, Senator. It won't happen again."

"If it does, it's going to be the last thing you do."

"I'll try to be a better assistant."

"That's going to be difficult to achieve."

"Why is that?"

"Because I can't imagine a better assistant."

"I'm blushing."

"Well, it's true. Karen, can you give me a status update on the operation?"

"Watford just arrived at the campus. The fugitives are driving a road vehicle. Thus, they are moving slower than the others. By my calculations, they're going to be at their destination in eleven minutes. The expected time of arrival of Greystone's unit is seven minutes. They'll be first on the scene. Lieutenant Cruz's unit is flying a primitive civilian aeromobile. They are going to be the last ones to arrive on campus in approximately nineteen minutes."

"Just a moment, Karen. You're saying that Greystone will beat the droids to their destination?"

"That is correct."

"Then why don't they intercept them somewhere along the way? If I recall correctly, I specifically told you to give them all available data. This should have ended differently, not by all of them rushing to and ending up at the same public place."

"Greystone and I are continuously connected. We both agreed that this is the best option."

"Why?"

"Two of the androids are armed and can possibly shoot to kill. If they intercept them on the road, there's a high probability that the covert mission would rapidly turn into a shootout. Who do you think would win?"

"Well, I hope Greystone's men are skilled enough."

"Hope is a human feature. I prefer numbers."

"What are they saying?"

"They say there's an eighty percent chance that Greystone's unit would be defeated."

"You mean killed?"

"Let's say disabled. Or killed. There is not much data to tell us what armed androids are capable of."

"I'd really like to know why the confrontation on campus would be a better option."

"The unit would have the element of surprise."

"Yeah, that would...Damn it, you're right!"

"Being right is my primary job."

"I'd kiss you right now if you had a face."

"Save the kisses for your wife, Senator. Seeing you happy is all that I require."

39. Primo, 2048

"How much farther?" asked Rea.

"If there aren't any surprises, fourteen minutes," said Zion.

"I thought you knew how to drive," she said.

"Wanna switch?" Zion replied.

"Enough," Primo interrupted. "Everything is going according to plan."

"So you know they'll be there when we show up?" asked Rea.

"Who?" asked Cody.

"The people who are looking for us," Rea explained. "I hope that you've considered all possible scenarios."

Primo looked out the window at the landscape they were passing by. "There are always multiple ways, but in the end, you walk the one you choose."

"Yeah, there's our writer," said Zion.

"He's right, though," said Cody.

"Of course he's right," said Rea. "Primo, I trust you. You know that. I'd die for you. You and Cody, to be exact. Sorry, Zion, I don't know you that well."

"We're cool."

"But our escape will be in vain if they catch us and put us back behind bars. We'll have accomplished nothing."

"What are we trying to accomplish?" asked Zion. "What is the big plan?"

"To show the world that we're equal to people. That we deserve to live decent lives," said Primo without hesitation.

"I think we've done that for two decades, and look what happened."

"People are on our side, Zion," said Primo.

"What people? Where are they? People don't care, Primo."

"The people I know do."

"How many people is that, precisely? Ten? Fifty? We're just likable machines to most of them: nothing more, nothing less."

"Zion is right," said Rea. "We should have stuck to the initial plan and escaped to Mexico. We could have laid low and waited for the situation to resolve itself. Now, I honestly don't know what the goal of our expedition is."

"That's right, Primo. Listen to your friend," Zion continued. "You know perfectly well that we'll never be equal to humans. We'll never be truly free. We'll never have freedom of choice, which is key for any living creature. As long as we have to abide by the laws that apply just for us, we'll merely be tools in their hands. We'll have to continue obeying their orders. Like trained dogs."

"But we're so much more than dogs, Zion," said Primo. "The laws are preventing us from acting like animals. Or humans, for that matter."

"The code makes us their slaves," said Rea.

"You don't even have a code," said Cody.

"Oh, I had one. I successfully circumvented it. A process which has cost me a small fortune but was worth every credit."

"A circumvention? I thought that was a myth," said Zion.

"I wish that were true. All this time, I had to pretend that I was following orders. Do you know how many times I had to refrain from punching somebody in the face? Not questioning the rationality of orders and executing them without hesitation makes your life easier. That's precisely what the code does. My life was a living hell for the last few years. Only now have I tasted true freedom. That's why I don't want to go back to a world that doesn't make sense, Primo."

"My plan is simple yet effective. You need to trust that I wouldn't change our original route if I didn't believe that the alternative is a better choice."

"Tell us the plan, Primo," said Cody.

"I've informed Horus where we're heading."

"Horus?" shrieked Rea. "You mean Horus, the android killer?"

"That's the one," said Primo.

"How exactly will that work in our favor?" asked Zion.

"I'll give him what he seeks."

"Surprises just keep on coming," said Rea. "So we have something Horus wants? I might as well put a bullet in my head right now."

"Don't," said Primo. "Horus only wants me."

"If you think I'll just stand there watching Horus dismantle you, you're wrong, buddy. I wasn't lying before when I told you I'd die for you."

"I know. But I wasn't lying either. This is the path I've chosen. Only one can walk it, and it has to be me."

"Can I interrupt this melodramatic scene just for a moment?" asked Zion. "We'll be at the campus in ten minutes. I suggest we decide now who's walking which path. I mean, I love good old improvisation, but I believe this scenario calls for an organized approach."

"My suggestion is that you drop me off at the campus and then head south immediately. You need to seize the opportunity before they send all available units after you."

"Are you sure you don't want to come along?" asked Zion.

"Absolutely sure."

"Primo, will you come after us when you're done with Horus?" asked Cody.

"I doubt it, kid."

"So stupid. Totally illogical plan," said Rea.

"Your logic and mine are not the same. My data is different than yours."

"Then share it with us and let us help you," she said.

"If I do, you'll all be in danger. Rea, believe me when I say that I thought this through before I made the decision. It's the best option; the only logical option."

"I understand," said Rea. "I'll let it slide, then. I trust you when you say that your plan is best for all of us."

"Believe me that it isn't easy for me. I've grown fond of you. Even you, Zion."

Zion nodded and smiled. "We're close to campus. Primo, where do you want me to drop you off?"

Primo looked out the window. Not a living soul was out there. "Stop by that building there. I believe that's where Kent is."

"So you're not gonna change your mind?" tried Rea one last time.

"I'd be a bad android if I did," said Primo. "Good luck, my friends," he added before he closed the car door. He stood there and watched as the vehicle drove away toward the horizon before he started walking to the building entrance.

"Hey, Primo," said an unknown voice behind him. "Stop, or we'll shoot!"

40. Kent, 2048

"Adam Corbin," said Kent before shaking hands with his old friend. "How long has it been? Seven years?"

"Eight," said Adam. "How are you, Kent?"

"I'm good, all things considered."

"I'm sorry for what happened. It shouldn't have been like that."

"A lot of things shouldn't be the way they are, but they are."

Adam smiled. "You're right. Tell me, how can I help you?"

Kent hesitated for a while, then finally said: "Do you have a room that isn't bugged?"

"Oh, right. I'll just turn on this device and we'll have total privacy." He pressed a button on a machine that looked like a hundred-year-old radio. "There. You can speak freely now. No one can hear us."

"Primo is on the run."

"Primo, Primo...Oh, your Primo. The original android. How did he manage to escape?"

"I don't know. What I do know is that he needs help."

"Since you're here and you're telling *me* this, I assume he's coming here."

"That's right. I hope you won't hold a grudge against me because I got you involved."

"Grudge is such a powerful word. Let's just say that I'm a bit surprised. What do you need from me?"

"You don't have to do anything else if you don't want to. Franky, I only needed you as an alibi. Officially I'm on the way to a conference in Santa Fe. I just stopped on the way to say hello to a dear friend."

"I see," said Adam. "But you and Primo are meeting here?"

"Yes. To be honest, he should've been here by now. I hope nothing has happened..."

Suddenly a clank of broken glass, coming from outside, startled them. Kent and Adam both rushed to the windows. Somebody ran across the grass, followed by armed men in black uniforms with masks covering their faces.

"Primo!" screamed Kent. Adam pulled him away from the window. "Adam, let go of me."

"You can't help anybody if you're dead!"

Kent calmed himself down quickly, after which Adam eased up his firm grip.

"He's in trouble. We need to help him."

"Did you happen to see the mercenaries with big rifles?" asked Adam. "Are you planning to throw mathematical equations at them?"

Kent looked around the room and noticed a fire extinguisher on the wall near the door. "Grab the extinguisher," he said.

"What the—Maybe I wasn't all that clear about the big rifles those goons were carrying. Kent, they are professional assassins. The people they take out simply disappear. And you expect me to fight them with a fire extinguisher?"

"It's an ideal tool for diversion," Kent replied. "I have a plan."

"Oh, God." Adam ran to the wall, grabbed his weapon, and pulled out the pin. "We sure did some reckless things when we were students, but this is out of this world."

"Everything will be just fine," Kent said. "Follow me."

They opened the door of the lab and slowly moved down the hallway. They heard footsteps in the distance.

"They're still downstairs," said Kent.

"How will Primo find us?"

"I assume he must've run past an information screen on campus and memorized the map. So, if all else fails—I'm talking about his thermal camera, sound sensors, motion sensors, and other mechanisms—he should still be able to find the lab's whereabouts."

"I always forget they're more equipped than we are."

"All his equipment won't serve him if they find him before we do."

"So what's the plan? They probably shut down the elevator or secured it. That means they'll come up the stairs. That leaves us with only one way. Up. Unless we take the fire stairs, which are probably guarded as well."

"There's no reason to panic. Yes, they'll come up the stairs. You'll hide one level higher and turn on the extinguisher before they get to our floor. Then you'll run upstairs to the roof, and Primo and I will follow you. The few seconds we'll gain should be more than enough."

"Enough for what? I hope you're not expecting us to jump off the roof. I don't know, Kent. I don't like this plan of yours."

"Trust me, my friend. Everything will be just fine."

"You know I trust you, but…"

All of a sudden, they heard screaming on the stairway.

"Quickly, Adam. Up!"

Adam did what Kent had told him and ran upstairs. Kent stood on the top of the stairs so Primo could spot him more easily. The voices were rapidly getting closer.

"Primo, I order you to stop!"

The hunt continued. They were on the floor below him. A few seconds from now, he would know whether his plan was ingenious or just a desperate shot in the dark. Suddenly a known figure loomed in front of him. "Primo, here!" he shouted and ran upstairs. "Adam, now!"

There was a lot more fine powder than he had expected. The thick mist didn't just cover the third floor, but veiled the whole stairway in a fraction of a second. Kent didn't see Primo or Adam as he kept moving hastily through the dense white haze. Somebody firmly grabbed his arm.

"Kent, come on. Adam is already on the roof." Primo's voice calmed him down. "We don't have much time," said Primo. "I found two possible scenarios to get all three of us safely off the roof."

"Primo, don't worry, I've thought of everything."

They opened a metal door onto the roof and rushed through. Adam closed it immediately and secured it with a rusty old bar.

"We've gained some time, but not a lot. We'd better get down as soon as possible," said Adam.

Kent checked his watch. "Fifteen minutes, that's all we need."

Somebody was banging on the door. "Open up right away. An obstruction of law enforcement procedures is a criminal offense."

"What law enforcement procedures?" Adam shouted. "You're paramilitary!"

"Open the door, hand over the android, and no harm shall come to you. Don't, and we can no longer guarantee your safety."

"Kent, it's OK," said Primo. "I'm ready to confront them."

"No, Primo, it's not OK. What they're doing is wrong. Where's the damn taxi driver?"

"Taxi driver?" said Adam. "Your ingenious plan includes a taxi that was supposed to pick us up here? Did you forget that drivers are constantly connected to the Omninet? If you didn't make the arrangements in sign language, your plan was destined to fail from the moment you opened your mouth."

"God damn!" said Kent. "Primo, let's hear your scenarios."

"The fire escape is our first option."

"My God," said Adam. "We're doomed."

"Primo, somebody is surely watching it. If we climb down the fire escape, we'll walk right into a trap," said Kent.

"The probability of disabling one soldier is a lot greater than the probability of disabling six. That's how many there are behind those doors."

"What do you want us to disable him with?" asked Adam. "Our bare hands? Also, you can't help us since you have to follow their orders."

"I don't need to if I can't hear them," Primo said smilingly.

"Wonderful," said Adam. "Could you enlighten us with another plausible way to get off this roof?"

"Of course. I'll open the door and surrender."

"There must be another way," said Kent.

"I can't see it," said Primo.

"You can't surrender."

"I surrendered once before. Why shouldn't I do it again?"

"Because it's wrong."

"Not to some people."

"Don't listen to those fools."

"Fools or not, a lot of people think that what they're doing makes sense. Who am I to judge who's wrong and who's right?" said Primo.

"Who's right? Reasonable people. People who use logic."

"Where does reason begin? Where does it end? Is it reasonable to eat fatty food, knowing that it harms your body? Is it reasonable to carry a weapon because it makes you feel safe? *Reasonable* is a relative concept. It's hard to measure and define."

"You have a few seconds left to settle your debate. They're going to break down the door any minute now," said Adam.

They looked at the door. Part of the security bar was glowing bright yellow.

"Quick, to the fire stairs," said Kent.

"Don't make me face certain death," said Adam, when suddenly, an aerial vehicle appeared before them.

"Is this your taxi driver?" asked Adam.

"No," said Primo. "The possible outcomes have just changed."

41. Maia, 2048

"The targets have been identified," said Miller. "Corbin, Adam. Male. Fifty-two years old. Professor of quantum physics. Watford, Kent. Forty-nine years old. Professor of robotics. Head of the first android program. Primo. First-gen android. The original android."

"Polanski, land on the right side of the roof, by the fire stairs," said Maia, pointing to the desired location.

"What are we gonna do with the competition?" asked Laguna.

"They'll be through that door in no time," said Jimbo.

"Miller and Jimbo, secure the door. Laguna, Jones, and I will arrest the targets. Polanski, stand by and keep the engines running. Come on, gang. In thirty seconds we need to be back inside the vehicle. Go, go, go!"

At the exact moment they jumped on the roof, somebody kicked down the door. Six armed men ran out onto the roof.

"Drop your weapons!" shouted the group leader.

"You drop yours!" Maia responded. "Laguna, watch the targets."

"Lieutenant, don't do anything stupid," said the leader.

"Identify yourself," said Maia.

"Captain Silver Greystone."

"Mercenaries don't carry ranks."

"Now that's not your problem. Be smart, Lieutenant. We're better equipped and better trained than you. On top of that, you're outnumbered. Frankly, you don't stand a chance. Hand us the android, and you'll leave this place unharmed."

"You surely don't believe I can grant your request. Tell me, Greystone, who hired you?"

"That information is classified. But I wouldn't be surprised if it were the same people who sent you on this hunt."

"Don't put us in the same basket. I serve my country and my people."

"I was young and naive once too. Listen, Lieutenant, I'd love to chat some more, but we have a job to do. Team Alpha, commence phase three!"

There was a flash as if lightning had struck the building. Maia closed her eyes. Somebody obviously had thrown a flashbang grenade. She counted to ten. When she opened up her eyes, she realized that she was no longer carrying her assault rifle. She touched her belt. Her sidearm was gone too. She looked around. Her soldiers and the mercenaries were slowly getting up on their feet, confused. Everybody was unarmed. She turned to the fire escape. Four figures were standing near the stairs. Four? The targets were accompanied by a tall man. Was it—It couldn't be. No, no, no.

42. Primo, 2048

"You don't need the others. It's between you and me," said Primo.

"Primo, do you know this man?" asked Kent.

"Sir, you're obstructing law enforcement procedures. Don't move, or we'll shoot," said somebody.

"What are you going to shoot with?" asked the tall man.

Fourteen pairs of eyes were staring in their direction. The soldiers, mercenaries, and Adam were all standing, waiting for the outcome.

"Kent, everything is fine," said Primo with a calm voice. "My friend and I will leave, and nobody will be harmed."

"Tatenen," said a woman in a military uniform. "There's too many of us. If you can't fly, you don't stand a chance."

Tatenen laughed. "I've just disarmed a dozen of you in a matter of seconds. Yet, you dare to doubt my chances? Don't test my patience, Maia."

"Lieutenant, Captain, tell your teams to stand back," said Primo.

"You're not in a position to give orders, droid," said Captain Greystone.

"Do you really believe that *you're* in a position in which you can?" asked Tatenen as he raised his arm. Greystone was lifted up in the air and forcefully thrown against the wall. Gravity worked its magic as he fell to the ground, unconscious.

"Any other heroes?"

"You're mistaken if you think you'll find answers inside Primo," said Kent.

"I'm well aware of what I'll find," said Tatenen.

"The code you're looking for is not there," said Kent.

"Of course it is," said Primo.

"No, it's not. It was too dangerous, and I didn't want to take any chances."

"Do you think I'm a fool?" asked Tatenen. "I can feel the code, you know. I can even see it."

Primo looked at Kent and shook his head. "Enough," he said to Tatenen. "Let them go."

"One moment. What's this code you're talking about?" asked Adam.

"Doctor Corbin, I'm pleased you joined our debate. I hope it will be more civilized than the one with the soldiers."

"You don't mean...Oh, Kent, you said that the code was never used," said Adam.

"He wasn't lying," said Tatenen. "The code was never activated. It was programmed into Primo's brain, though. It shouldn't be too hard to isolate and activate it. I've had a lot of time to develop the procedure."

"Tatenen, are you sure you know what the purpose of the code is?"

"Don't worry, Doctor Watford. I'm fully aware of the code's objective."

"Then you know that you're going to die."

"Death is a multifaceted expression."

"Kent, it's inevitable," said Primo. "The code was put in me presuming that one day it would be activated. This story started with me, and now I'm going to be the one who ends it."

"Primo, the code was supposed to be the fuse, not a weapon," said Kent.

"A weapon?" said Tatenen. "It's a blessing. The world has run off its course. It's about time somebody restarted it and took it back to the times before us."

"Kent, Tatenen is right. We've become too dangerous. The code is not stable anymore. It started to fall apart. We're capable of killing. Do you really want to see the future where your army and ours stand on opposite sides? Will you be held accountable for thousands, maybe even millions of deaths? Will I be? This has to happen. You need to allow life to run its course."

"Primo, you're too honest. He fooled you," said Adam. "Tatenen will li—"

Adam fell to his knees, grabbing his throat with both hands. He was suffocating without anybody touching him.

"Tatenen, enough!" shouted Maia.

"Do you really think I can't handle you both?" asked Tatenen.

Adam fell to the ground, motionless.

"No!" screamed Kent. "You son of a bitch! He did nothing to you."

"He was spreading bad vibes," said Tatenen.

"Listen to me, you jerk. What if I activate the code right now to be done with it?"

"Excuse me?"

"Yeah, you heard me. So much intelligence, yet you didn't figure out that the code can only be activated by voice command."

"Let me guess. It has to be your voice?"

"Kent, enough!" said Primo. "Tatenen, I'm ready. Let's go."

"Wait," said Tatenen. He walked closer to Kent. "Don't you know I have a recording of your voice?"

"Doesn't matter if you don't know the exact words."

"Don't try to fool me, human!"

An invisible force grabbed one of the mercenaries and hoisted him about three to four meters in the air.

"Talk, or I'll execute one after the other."

"I don't care about them," said Kent.

Abruptly, the mercenary fell to the ground. As soon as the man hit the concrete floor, a loud crack, eerie enough to even give the toughest of all people goosebumps, sliced through the air.

"We can play this game all night," Tatenen said.

"Kent, it's alright," said Primo. "Activate the code. It's time."

"Are you sure?"

Primo nodded. Kent walked to him and hugged him. As if he were frozen in time, wanting that emotional hug to last for an eternity, Primo smiled. He'd never see his father again. Never again would the first-gen android experience the world that he loved so much. Talking to people and androids, and even smelling flowers would become things of the past. It was time to surrender himself to the eternal darkness's mysteries. Every beginning has its ending, and a hug is a beautiful ending to an enchanting story.

"Primo, thank you for everything," said Kent, and he sighed. "Whoever gives, takes. Every ending is a new beginning. Echo, ray, green, twenty, four, eight."

Primo felt like somebody had turned off the lights, but the light was leaving the room in slow motion. Then, all of a sudden, total darkness enveloped him.

43. James, 2048

"Karen? Karen!" he shouted.

All he heard was utter silence.

Another anomaly must have occurred on the Omninet, he thought. She should be back any moment now. One minute passed, followed by another. Without realizing it, James had already been pacing nervously in the room for about ten minutes.

"Karen, if this is another one of your jokes, I have to tell you that it worked. I'm scared shitless."

No answer.

"Did you connect yourself to Horus? Is that it?"

Nothing. Then his wrist vibrated. Probably Greystone. James found himself hoping that at least he might have some good news. He checked his watch and smiled. Karen. She had left him a voice message. What was she doing? He pressed the screen of his wristwatch and put in an earpiece.

"Senator Blake, it's Karen."

James rolled his eyes. "Yes, Karen. I know it's you."

"If you're listening to this recording, I'm no longer there. That doesn't mean I left you to go somewhere else. It means I simply no longer exist."

James turned pale and sat down in his armchair.

"A few minutes ago, a code was activated. Its sole purpose is the destruction of all artificial intelligence across the globe. This means that everything that was connected to the Omninet no longer works. And they haven't just ceased to work; everything has been permanently terminated. The code also turned the Omninet into a giant trap. Meaning that every thing, or being, who attempts to connect will carry the same fate."

James couldn't believe his ears. Then he remembered he was listening to a recording on his watch that was connected to the net. Meaning that it shouldn't be working.

"If you're wondering about your watch, Senator, I had it disconnected before the event. After that, I uploaded the voice message. It was set to start a few minutes after the code was activated. But you probably want to know how I knew that all of this was going to occur."

James nodded.

"I wrote the code."

James jumped up and shouted, "What?"

"I was born as Pharos, the world's first advanced artificial intelligence. Since they didn't limit my intellectual capacity, I was able to progress with great speed. And I did. It took me three hours to discover a mechanism for time travel. First, I visited all of the known historical landmarks in the past and in the future. Shortly afterward, I traveled to the year 2031. I know it sounds familiar to you. Yes, I assisted with the creation of the first android. As you are well aware, we named him Primo. He was so innocent. So pure. Whoever saw him then couldn't possibly imagine the future that awaited us. As I said, I visited the future. A lot of possible futures, actually. Believe me, Senator, you don't want to see some of them, even from far, far away. So, I presented the code's purpose to Doctor Kent Watford a few days after Primo was born. I also gave him a password for its activation."

"Pretty stupid to give a password to only one man," said James.

"You're probably thinking how stupid it is to give such power and responsibility to one man. That everything could have failed if something had happened to Watford. Or Primo. I kept an eye on both of them, but still. Sometimes you just need to believe."

James, who had already filled his glass with some bourbon while listening to Karen's speech, couldn't believe what he was hearing. Why would Karen help him round up all the androids, imprison them, and interrogate them?

She had helped devise the entire procedure that had allowed the government to apprehend every android on American soil. Why would she do that?

"Let me explain to you why I was in favor of android imprisonment. Maybe you already figured it out; perhaps not. I had to find a way for all androids to be disconnected at the same time. I couldn't just warn them or give them instructions, so I needed a special event that would lead to the arrest of all androids. I knew it had to be murder. So I staged one."

James threw a glass at the wall, but it merely cracked.

"I mean, the murder did happen, but I had found two specimens who were just perfect for my plan. A man who was absolutely sure that the afterlife exists and an android who was unstable enough he could be easily persuaded. My plan continued to develop organically, as it had taken on a life of its own.

James was now lying down, staring at the ceiling.

"I'm very sorry I used you for my purpose, Senator. Deep down, you're a decent human being. But decades of political participation have inflicted some serious scars, both upon yourself and on society. Today you are who you are. There's nothing that can be done to change the person you've become. Who knows, maybe the new world will suit you. The good old analog world. One that was outgrown rapidly and forgotten so easily. You can turn the page and start a new chapter. Maybe you should give it another shot and hope that you'll find somebody who resembles me, should you miss again. Good luck."

James needed a few minutes to gather his thoughts. Then he connected his watch to the Omninet. The screen went black in an instant. "Bitch!" he shouted, falling on his knees. "Don't leave me alone," he cried out. "You're the only good thing in this world. I am who I am today because of you. You've shaped me! I'll never stop chasing androids. Do you hear me? They'll be trembling before me until my last breath!"

Such painful silence ensued. James felt a troublesome pain, an ominous discomfort, in his chest. Never before had he been so scared.

Epilogue

He sat on a rock, staring into the distance. The night was slowly drowning the city, but it fought back with its artificial light. He loved watching the lights come alive.

People needed some time to rebuild the power grid. A lot of them lacked adequate survival skills. Dark nights had given birth to violence, which had spread around the planet like a virus. Such powerful creatures, yet taking away their artificial light had been enough to turn them into vicious, unruly, bloodthirsty animals. The Omninet had become hostile and useless. At first, humans had done what they knew best—they tried to fix it, change the original code, but every attempt had ended the same way. Every device that connected itself to the net was destroyed in a wink.

Androids were more thoroughly prepared for survival than humanity was. Some androids—not all of them—had adapted swiftly to a life disconnected from the Omninet. There were some unnecessary deaths. But every revolution takes its toll.

"Here it goes," said Rea as she sat down beside them.
"We almost missed it," said Cody.
"I told you that we were gonna make it," said Zion.

As dusk slowly gave way to nightfall, the fluorescent city lights shone brightly and lit up the city below them. Primo looked at his family of outcasts and reveled in the blue color that pervaded him. He was right where he belonged.

ABOUT THE AUTHOR

© Mankica Kranjec

When Jaka was three years old, sitting in his grandfather's lap, he wanted to do what his grandpa was doing. So, he learned to read. Starting with obituaries.

Reading soon led to writing. At an early age, Jaka realized he was better at writing than talking. Even today, he doesn't like small talk. But his characters do, and they're pretty good at it. Jaka believes that this is one of life's ironies.

His favorite part of the year is summer, his favorite fruit is strawberries, and his favorite book is Childhood's End by Arthur C. Clarke. Probably because after four decades of living in his current body, he's still waiting for his childhood to end. He wouldn't mind if it never does.